Midnight Looks Good on You

Kyler Jones

ISBN: 978-0-578-83033-9

Acknowledgments

To my parents, John and Toni. Thank you.

To my grandma, who passed away during the writing of this book. You are missed.

To my friends Devon Hewett (the writer) and Juan Bruno (the scholar). Your support means the world.

And to the more than three hundred million worldwide who deal with depression. Know that you are not alone, and even though things may be dark right now…

I think the midnight looks good on you.

Table of Contents

The Parlor

6:01 p.m.

Andrew Harper opened his eyes and was blinded by the white-hot glare of the California sun peeping through the apartment window blinds. Everything hurt like hell—especially his head. Every time he blinked, bombs and grenades went off like wartime.

The actor's North Hollywood apartment was a shitshow. Burger wrappers, beer bottles, and dust bunnies littered the floor. Not to mention a couple of smoking bowls and lighters on the coffee table.

And the greasy-haired twentysomething with a pair of watermelon tits on the sofa next to him. The girl was snoring like thunder, and there was cigarette ash all over her lap. From what he remembered, they'd drunk enough the night before to take down a rhino.

Andrew looked over and admired the pink streak in Natasha's hair. No doubt done by some alt-rocker boyfriend or sleazy West Hollywood tattoo artist. Her usual type. "Natasha, get up!" he spat, jarring the girl out of her hazy slumber. Her eyes popped open like a pair of jack-in-the-box toys, followed by a creaky attic groan.

"I feel like death reincarnate," she said, somehow mustering the strength to push herself up and reach for a dirty glass bong and Bic lighter on the coffee table. She took two hits and passed the paraphernalia to Andrew, who did the same but wheezed, hacking out a lungful of green goop in the process. "If you die, do I get the apartment?" Natasha laughed while wiping crusts of yellowy sleep from her eyes.

But Andrew only frowned, feeling every bit of his fifty-two to her twenty-four now. A lot of actors dreamed of having younger groupies. The only irony was he'd picked the one with the biggest mouth in Hollywood.

So there was that to deal with.

"You know what? At least I'm not shacking up with some guy old enough to be my father." Andrew snickered, remembering the jokes and jests they'd shared the night before.

"Ouch. Go take a shower, old man. You stink." Natasha stuck her tongue out.

"Yeah, well, your future stinks," Andrew spat back. He wobbled onto both feet with the sturdiness of a toddler on a pogo stick.

"I'm going to art school in the fall."

"Oh, sure you are, sweetie. And you're getting a job too—and your own place, and Jesus is coming back from the dead!"

Andrew liked Natasha. She was quirky and liked to talk back and give him shit. Playful little jabs to the gut about his career, aging looks (even though she preferred older men), and relevancy. Even though she was twenty-four and a nobody. But that was the city of Hollywood. The industry spat people out like tobacco chew.

Andrew did shower, though, after eventually gathering the strength to wobble over to the bathroom and flip the faucet on. He let the hot water run down his achy shoulders, back, and legs.

And after showering, he wrapped a towel around his body, wiped smudges of steam from the mirror with his palm, and looked at himself long and hard in the mirror, cringing at every crinkle, hard divot, and discoloration on his weathered face.

When he trotted back into the living room, Natasha was still on the couch, but now she'd flipped the TV on and was watching a movie. An old 1981 slasher flick called *The Prowler*. The one about a masked killer (but weren't they all) who wears a military outfit and jabs attractive teenagers with a bayonet.

Andrew knew of the film, and he knew the film's director, Joseph Zito, too. Back in the day, they'd almost produced a film together, some indie scream teen flick about a haunted carnival called *Blood Games*. (The script was about as good as the title, though.)

"You keep watching that shit, your brain will turn to mush, darling," Andrew cackled.

But Natasha didn't care. Instead, she offered a tasty middle finger and a grin. "Says the man who depends on mush to support himself now."

"Oh. Way to gut a man's ego, Nat."

"Are you taking me to Horror-Con this year? I wanna go."

"I don't know, it depends if they're doing a Q&A again. That way I get paid regardless. Depending on autographs and merch sales is too risky."

"Hmm. OK. I really wanna meet Robert Englund." Natasha reached for the bong again.

"Fuck Robert Englund."

"Yeah, I know, right? I totally would. For a grandpa, he's pretty hot."

"Christ. What laboratory concocted you?"

Andrew rolled his eyes and settled into the couch. He knew horror fans were a different breed of human. Usually oddballs with too much time on their hands—or gothy-looking young girls with black eye makeup and daddy issues, like Natasha. It was the reason events like Horror-Con existed. Or that older genre actors like Andrew even had a speck of relevancy some twenty years on. The love of the genre bordered on undying lust for millions of fans.

Andrew leaned over and swiped his meaty arm around Natasha, pulling her in close to him. In one corner of his mind, he thought about popping a few Advil and a Viagra and downing a cup of coffee to get her in bed again. But in the other, he wanted to give the girl twenty dollars to go to the corner store and buy another case of beer. "Why don't you do me a favor, sweetie? My wallet's on the counter. Pick us up some dinner and a case of beer for tonight."

Natasha's face morphed to a pouty frown. Now the TV was off, and so was her attitude. "Don't call me that."

"Call you what?"

"Sweetie. It's so degrading. And get your hand off my thigh."

"Oh Christ. You know what I mean. Don't be one of those cranky millennials."

"Cranky *what*? Dude. Last night was fun, but don't be rude—and I'm not your slave. My head hurts. If you want booze that bad, go get it yourself."

"Hey, calm your tits!"

"You're the one screaming at me."

"Oh, forget it. You bitch!" Andrew snapped, slamming his heel into a couple empty bottles of Coors Light and Budweiser strewn about the messy floor.

"Wow! Bitch, huh? Okay, fuck you. I'm leaving."

"Oh why's that? So you can go home and tell your dad you fucked his favorite film star?" Andrew bopped another beer can on the floor with his foot.

"'Film star?' Ha! Please! Not since I was learning to color inside the lines." Natasha smirked, lifting her foot up and kicking the bong off the table, where it dropped like a rocket and shattered all over the floor in a scatter bomb of glass.

"You fucking BITCH! Get the fuck out!" Andrew hollered until his lungs hurt, catapulting the girl across the living room. Thumping through even more hoards of cans, squashed cigarettes, and other piles of bullshit to get there.

After Andrew kicked her out, he rammed the door shut. And then, using both fists, began walloping it in a blinding rage. Pow. Pow. Pow.

Thirty minutes later, the actor was downing bathroom cabinet mouthwash for the buzz.

***

He spent that evening hopping from one favorite bar to the next. Jeremiah's on Sunset for bourbon, then The Federal on Wilshire for tequila, and finally El Ton, a Mexican margarita joint in North Hollywood, for a round of cold beers. Andrew's '08 pearl-black Audi kept up all right, though.

Some cars are better bender machines than others.

Around eleven, Andrew cracked the driver's-side window to light a cigarette. He alternated between cup of coffee and cigarette with relative ease, all the while keeping one firm grip on the wheel. Thanks to a couple of Advil and a coffee/bourbon mixer, his head wasn't pounding anymore. Only thumping marginally like a beginner's drum kit.

But when he saw it, he saw it. Like spotting a tick on a dog. If Andrew had zipped by any quicker, he would've missed it. But tonight, for whatever reason, he noticed it…

Massage parlors are a common occurrence in larger cities like Los Angeles. But Andrew, like many other males his age, knew the dark truth. Most of the independently owned parlors substituted for brothels or pay-to-play sex clubs. He should know—he'd frequented most of the clubs in the North Hollywood and Van Nuys area.

For a Los Angeles parlor, however, this one was different. It had no flashy dancing "Open" sign hanging on the front window to let all the mongrels and monsters of the city know who was open for business. And the parking lot looked more Mad Max than masturbator command center.

There were soda pop bottles and balled-up tissue paper strewn everywhere. And there was one overstuffed trash bin filled with junk, probably the odd bullet casing, a junkie needle, and a couple of marijuana dispensary capsules—stuff like that.

Still, something, an unknown force tempted Andrew to whip in for himself. That was its magic power. *I bet the damn thing's not open anyway*, he thought, hopping out of his car with the enthusiasm of a boy about to do something naughty.

The thrill and rush of paying for sexual gratification never got old. Andrew's adrenaline always peaked before the orgasm, and for good reason. Of all of the hedonistic ways to spend one's life—abusing alcohol, drugs, and women—there was nothing quite like the temptation of the flesh.

Andrew trotted up to the parlor's front door, a big, fat, fuck-you sloppy smile slapped on his face. He was feeling great. No, more than great. Like he was about to take part on an adventure. And his cock was the boost rocket ready to rock him into orbit.

When he opened the parlor door, a tiny bell went off, and an older Asian woman, maybe sixty but no taller than five foot two, whipped around the corner. Smiling. "Ello, mister, first time?" she said, her accent doing loop-de-loops around each syllable.

"Here. Yeah, it is," Andrew quipped. hoping to God this old bitch wasn't the "masseuse."

"One hundred fifty dolla for one hour. Or eighty for half. You pay now. Tip later," the old woman muttered, her body stiff as a board.

Andrew cackled. "A hundred fifty? You're joking." He could toss a random lawn dart at any parlor in Los Angeles, and it would be under one hundred. Hell, even seventy.

The woman didn't seem to mind his outburst. Instead, she hollered out something in another language. Mandarin? Andrew couldn't be sure.

But that didn't matter because, one second later, a pair of beautiful young Asian women materialized like a magic trick. And they were topless. Their perfectly shaped breasts, round and pointed like cones, jiggled with each step. One even appeared to be sucking on her finger like a lollipop.

Andrew's jaw automatically unhinged and dropped to the floor while his penis did the opposite—pushing onto his zipper hard enough to hurt good. He knew the whole slut act wasn't anything special, just another fishing lure to bring in promiscuous men. And rip them off.

But by God, it worked like a charm.

The older Asian woman smirked. "You pay now."

Andrew reached for his wallet and whipped out two hundred-dollar bills. (All he had left for the month's groceries, but fuck it.) He said, "I want them both," and winked. The fuel of his libido was unstoppable now. How many men had been pleasured here? A hundred? Two hundred? Or a thousand perhaps? All of them searching for the same sick sexual satisfaction. And now it was Andrew's turn to ride the bull.

The actual parlor "room" was small, with pink rose wallpaper and violin music drifting from a pair of wall speakers to set the mood. There was a massage table with no sheet smack dab in the center of the room, and a wash rack behind it that included a sink, hand towel cubby, and various lotion bottles.

"You undress—lay on table. Girls be in to deal with you shortly." The old woman bowed before disappearing back behind a thick velvet curtain. Nothing more than a shadow of a memory now.

To deal with me shortly. Huh. I like the sound of that. Andrew grinned, quickly chucking his clothing on the floor—shirt, pants, underwear, socks, and shoes. Then he lay face down on the table, every inch of his naked body exposed. The rush of revealing oneself to a stranger was more satisfying than any twenty-something groupie staying at his place. Andrew loved being seen and heard. It was the reason he got into acting in the first place.

From behind the curtain: "Okay, ready?" However, this voice was different, and did not seem to belong to the older woman. It was soft and delicate, like a purple flower blooming in the spring. The voice was one a man would kill to make love to.

The lights dimmed. One of the two beautiful women (this one black eyed and black haired, not the lollipop sucker) emerged like a mermaid from the depths, bent over, and lifted his chin up with a seductive finger.

"Where's the other woman? I paid for a four-handed massage." Andrew smirked, elevating himself up on both elbows, basking in the glory of what was to come.

However, the beautiful dark-haired woman only shook her head once and giggled, swinging around on one foot in a ballerina's twirling motion, dancing to the beat of her own drum.

"Okay." He laughed. "Sure, babe. I'm cool with this. Just as long as I get a piece of both of you."

But as he reached up to stroke her hand, she playfully pushed him away, waving the same finger back and forth in a "no" move.

"Oh, you like to play hard to get. Is this what you do, then? You strip a man down and bounce him around like a yo-yo. That's a dangerous game you play, girlie."

He almost got off the table, propelling himself up onto all fours—when another pair of foreign hands pushed him back down. One pressed into his spine, and the other latched onto a buttock. "Woah!" he exhaled, flipping around to find himself face-to-face with the other young woman. Ms. Lollipop from before.

"Well, hey there, honey? So how's this going down?" Andrew licked his lips, unable to lie flat on his stomach anymore because of his erect penis. He flipped over to help himself out.

But the girls weren't having that either.

"You turn back over. We scrub you with hot oil and rocks first," Lollipop smacked. Her broken English rebounded off the walls.

"Huh?" Andrew hiccupped, not sure whether to applaud the joke or not.

"Turn over."

“Ah Christ, I don’t actually want a fucking massage. You get me,” Andrew growled, only to get another tap on the shoulder from Ms. Dark and Sensual. The Black Beauty. Who was holding a bottle of liquid lotion in one hand and a Magnum condom in the other. A sort of psychosexual balancing act for the ages.

“Massage first. And then, fun time,” Lollipop quipped. Her face was rock-solid serious. No joke. No flirtation trick. Andrew sensed the change in temperature too. Things weren’t fun or sexy anymore, or carefree and aloof. It was clear who was in charge—and who wasn’t.

“Ok, yeah sure, ladies. Whatever.” He exhaled and rolled back over onto his stomach, letting Lollipop and Black Beauty go to work. Which they did. While Lollipop worked his thigh muscles and legs, Beauty conjured up some magic upstairs. Soft hands slipping and sliding up/down every bump and divot. And while it wasn’t what he’d initially wanted, Andrew was eventually able to relax and get into it.

After half an hour, one of the girls tapped him on the shoulder again, her delicate finger tracing the hard bone carelessly. “Okay, now we have big surprise for you, sir.”

Andrew lifted his head up and grinned again, full of vigor and joy, happy to know what was coming next. “Oh, I bet you do.” He chuckled to himself as he heard one of the girls walk out of the room.

“What do you do?” a voice (that he knew belonged to Lollipop) murmured, obviously vying for some small talk.

“Oh. I’m an actor,” Andrew said, his head still on the table, eyes shut.

“Mm. Movies?”

"Some old horror films from the 80s. I'm sorta…retired now. More producing, that type of stuff."

"Ohhhh, big powerful man. Lots of stature," Lollipop replied while continuing to stroke his back with playful little rubs.

"Uh, sure. Hey, where's your friend—"

The curtain opened up, and Black Beauty shuffled back into the room, giggling under her breath.

Actually, both of the girls were giggling now. Their joyous fits came out in subtle hisses like an air valve being flipped on.

"What's so funny, huh?" Andrew recoiled, turning over quicker than an egg under the sun. As he did, he saw Black Beauty holding a picnic-in-the-park type of ice chest. With a cream white birthday cake rim around the top lid. The sight was so bizarre, so out of place that all he could do was laugh too. "Okay. This is the weirdest foreplay I've ever been a part of."

"Shh. Put your head on the table, sir—or our session is over," Lollipop snapped. already wiping the lotion off the palms of her hands in haste.

Andrew had no idea why he obeyed, but he did.

And waited. First, he heard the sound of a lid (the ice box) being popped open. And then, the sound of someone's hands digging around in the ice box. Scraping ice. Searching for…something.

Fuck, this is weird. Andrew thought back on the other parlors he'd frequented. Remembering that sometimes the girls dove into their box of tricks if the guy was willing to play…

Until a new set of hands went to work on him. Hands with fat, stubby, sausage fingers and hairy knuckles. Hands that did clearly not belong to a woman.

Andrew's eyes flew open. Right on time for a fist to wallop him right in the face. *Smack.* Sending an array of dizzying kaleidoscope stars across his sight.

Then, the hairy-knuckled hands began to wrench him by the neck. Pulling, tugging, and twisting like someone attempting to unscrew the lid of a mayonnaise jar. Andrew lashed out with a kick. Flailing, fighting, hollering at the top of his lungs to no avail. As his head was quickly—by some alien brute force strength—being torn off.

The moment the naked man's head popped off like a Barbie doll's, Lollipop and Black Beauty turned to one another and shrieked with joy, their naked bouncy breasts and faces covered in blood and gore.

Just like the pair of hands from the icebox.

The barbarian man hands weren't their own, of course, but made from real skin, bone, and hairy things that fit on nicely like winter gloves. Lollipop scooped up Andrew's head and held it proudly like a momma bear cradling her cub, overcome with emotion.

A moment later, however, the parlor curtain parted, and the older Asian woman walked in, clutching a rusty iron cleaver in one hand and a foot-high stack of towels in the other.

"Very good, ladies. But be quick with the cleanup. We have company coming," she rattled off in Chinese, her words machine gun bullet fire. She handed Lollipop the cleaver and Beauty the towels.

It took one hour for the girls to hack apart Andrew's body. Severing all of his limbs—the arms, the legs, and the limp penis—with the cleaver. Ripping him apart like a vulture. Until finally, he was rolled into wads of plastic sandwich wrap and bagged like deli meat at the supermarket.

***

Outside in the parlor's parking lot, the midnight moon beamed down on the ladies' heads, illuminating their faces in a jolly glow. Los Angeles during the witching hour is a dead ringer for Hell. A apocalyptic sin city with empty streets and heavy hearts.

When the $100,000 black Mercedes with tinted windows and bulletproof lining whipped itself into the lot, though, nobody budged. Even after its headlights flipped off and a figure in a black suit and combed-back hair stepped out. Mr. Mercedes was tall, thin, and what most women would describe as devilishly handsome. And although he appeared to be an American male, Mr. Mercedes spoke in perfect Chinese. "Pick-up to go."

"Yes. We were having trouble finding a man, but luckily one came in at the last minute," the older woman, head owner and overseer of Los Angeles Fresh Meat butchery, replied in her native tongue as she handed over the food order.

"Well, good. It would have been a shame to go elsewhere. You ladies have served our community for many years, and we're very grateful." Mr. Mercedes reached into his jacket pocket and whipped out a fat envelope with rubber-banded green bills. "This is for the food. Take care."

He got back in his car and drove away.

Midnight Looks Good on You

The Killer

It started raining around seven. Heavy, hard drops fell like bombs on the sidewalk. But The Killer with the pistol in his bag, did not flinch; he maneuvered between the raindrops with the grace of a dancer.

Moscow is cold in the winter. But the city dwellers know how to handle the extreme weather well. It's the tourists that are the most uncomfortable; they behave like aliens from another planet.

Over twelve million people live within the city limits, seventeen million within the urban area. Moscow is where the thinkers and doers coexist, a melting pot of intelligence and muscle that makes it the brain of Russia.

The city is mainly supported by a large transit network, which includes four international airports, railways, and a monorail system, the Moscow Metro, which is the third largest monorail system in the world. Despite its influence on the world, the city is overpopulated, which allows for an underground of drugs, prostitution, and...murder.

Everywhere The Killer looked, people scrambled for cover, fleeing the rain with vast strides and quick arms.

The first time he murdered somebody, it was during a rainstorm. He thrust the steak knife into the victim's gut so hard that it broke off at the handle. And then he dragged the body out into the street and let Mother Nature wash away his sin. When blood mixes with water, the two dilute into one big messy mural painting of colors and swishes.

The Killer hated the word "murderer." Murderers were people that made the FBI's most- wanted list. Freaks that stored cadavers under the floorboards and drank virgin blood. Bundy, Gacy, the Hillside Strangler, and Zodiac.

He was a contract killer; he only killed for money. And he never killed women or children. To think that someone would murder for fun made him ill, made him feel like giving up on humanity. In his long career, though, he'd met a few psychos. The ones that did not mind wrapping wires around a child's throat or pushing pregnant women in front of trains. Also, the violent nature of The Killer's profession tended to drive people mad. Many of his colleagues thought they were gods—a Zeus who traded in a lightning bolt for a sniper scope.

Every contract killer thrives in the shadows, all the while hacking and slashing their way around the world like they're in one bold and beautiful horror movie. The lifestyle is extremely dangerous…but it pays well. And whoever stays (or doesn't die) on the roller coaster ride through all of its twists, turns, backflips, and vomit-inducing spins will become wealthier beyond their wildest dreams once the time comes to retire.

However, the fact that The Killer was still alive *and* sane after all years was special. A rarity. And his stable sanity made him unique. An auteur. He'd seen the job turn some people into PTSD-filled loons doomed by their demented nightmares. Those types always retired and had mental breakdowns. Then, you'd flip the television on and see them perched up in a clock tower somewhere, rifle in hand, screaming belligerent shit, with a swarm of cops and news trucks down below.

The Killer was gifted, no doubt about it. He still had no problem remaining calm during hailstorms of gunfire or in one-on one, hand-to-hand combat with some of the toughest soldiers in the world. To put it simply, he was born for the lifestyle.

But The Killer was not stupid. He saw the grey wisps in his beard and atop his head. More and more every day, it seemed. Old age has a way of creeping in like a lover's embrace.

When The Killer did die, the end would be quick, though: a human cannon ball shot out of the life pod. He thought about his own mortality every time he took a life. Questions crossed his mind like, *If Hell is real, will I burn forever?* or *Will I be forgiven for the sins I've committed?*

He knew he rode the line between good and evil like a unicycle circus performer balancing on the high wire. But when he did die, whenever and however that'd be, if the devil's hot knuckles rapped on his door, he would answer.

And no doubt The Killer would see visions of all the violence he'd painted. Flying bullets, slit throats, and booby-trapped explosives. And all of the funerals of all the men he'd murdered, their corpses perched up in sugar-brown coffins, waving skeletal hands.

"So long," they'd tell him, the rotting flesh dripping off their fingertips like hot mozzarella cheese. "See you down in the meat, rat fucker." And if Heaven and Hell did exist, well, The Killer would no doubt be shackled to the cave wall in Satan's lair.

The Killer imagined it that way. Every limb in his body would shiver and shake with fear, with unmistakable horror. He'd see pitchforks and hot well pits filled with bright orange fire for miles. If he cried out, Satan would only lick the salty tears off his cheeks with a pointed tongue.

And laugh harder.

The Night Ride

The Moscow job was simple, unlike its bastard weather. A hit. One man, one bullet, one life taken with the pull of a trigger.

Boom. The Killer had done hundreds just like it. Only this time, the payday was colossal. Quite possibly the largest sum of money he would ever be given to kill someone.

The reason was the risk. This time, there was no information on the target or job. He had been given a first-class ticket to Russia and told to lie low. Nothing more.

Usually, The Killer would be given a thick dossier in which there would be a typed-out bio of the target. Their family, friends, any wives or mistresses, their hobbies, location of work, their salary, the car they drove, and so on.

Everything.

The Killer always studied the dossier like homework. He liked to think that by the time he'd finished studying, he knew the target well enough to finish their sentences. It wasn't uncommon to dream about them too. Every tiny detail about that person was sucked into the black hole vortex The Killer nicknamed his brain. And then—and only then—did he feel confident enough to carry out the kill. To end a stranger's life.

A stranger—because that's what they were. Yeah, he knew the life facts, but that couldn't replace the flesh-and-blood memories that lifelong lovers, friends, and family have with someone.

In reality, no one deserved to die like this, at the hands of a gun for hire. The Killer wished that, in a perfect world, everyone would find the love of their life and live till ninety. But that's not how life worked. It was cold and heartless, like a boxer hungry for the title. And people were greedy and stupid. Most of the people he killed owed or had stolen money. A lot of them were also on the run or in hiding somewhere. A big part of The Killer's job was tracking them down.

Detective *and* marksman. A renegade Sherlock Holmes with a passion for gunplay.

But when The Killer found them, he could tell immediately who was afraid to die. The career criminals always accepted their fate. They were the ones bad from birth. People like that lived their lives on the outside. They enjoyed taking from others. It was the thrill, a rush. Better than any heroin hit or Las Vegas prostitute.

Other types of people pleaded for mercy. They were the ones that truly had something to live for, the ones he felt pity for, and ending their lives gave him great pain. A lot were family men. Good fathers and husbands behind on child support bills or taking care of a sick wife.

And money did not grow on trees.

Drug running was the express lane into riches. More money meant a better life with less stress and more smiles. Like affording a bigger house, a good car, better food, and diapers for the baby. Nothing extravagant like Scarface's million-dollar mansion with tabletops of cocaine and scantily clad hookers. Just the basic human needs.

So when someone like that took off with the money and ran, he felt sorrow. Some days, The Killer wished he could step into a time machine and talk them out of taking their employer's money. Just for the sake of their family's future and for a child that'd grow up in a dysfunctional household. No more family dinners, vacations, or important life events like watching their children grow up, graduate, marry the love of their life, and become parents too. The Killer snuffed all that out like a birthday candle. Poof.

He hated tearing families apart—but someone had to die. Someone always has to die.

Those were the rules.

If the target was a family man, sometimes The Killer let them (while held at gunpoint, of course) call their husband/wife/child and say goodbye. On one occasion (and only one), he allowed someone to finish their meal before he shot them between the eyes. But a gesture like that was rare, like an Earth-ending asteroid shooting through the stars.

While on assignment, The Killer's favorite weapon was the Glock 17—a machine pistol with a sound suppressor. The weapon held over thirty rounds and could easily stop an elephant in the middle of a stampede. If The Killer wanted to avoid attention, something like a garrote wire was popular, though he could turn anything into a weapon if needed.

For instance, ten years ago, smack dab in the middle of a crowded New York City subway platform, The Killer jabbed the end of a toothbrush through a target's eyeball. It was creative. Morbid. Something a horror writer like Stephen King would be proud of. The memory still made him chuckle from time to time.

This Russia job was odd indeed, nothing like the New York one. But the payday was monumental. A hundred and fifty thousand. Triple what he usually earned per assignment. People in The Killer's profession referred to these types of jobs as "Night Rides," named after the popular adolescent game where one person (usually some pimple-faced teenager) would turn off the car headlights and drive blindly down the road, laughing like a drunken warlord.

And of course, the high level of secrecy needed (for the assassination of a celebrity or political figure, perhaps) meant that Night Rides were extremely dangerous—but paid more than any other job.

Above The Killer's head, the moon kissed the dirty clouds and sky with a fever tongue. At the same time his plane touched Moscow tarmac, a black Mercedes with tinted bulletproof windows rolled up to Terminal 1.

No one got out of the car.

The Killer hadn't brought much: only a gym bag with some rolled-up shirts, pants, and a pair of boots. But tucked into one of the shirts were a Glock pistol and a hunting knife. Because of a special lining in the gym bag, the weapons got by metal detectors and scanners with ease.

A thin man with dagger-sharp cheekbones poked his head out the Mercedes's driver's-side window. He was older than The Killer, but not by much—early fifties, judging by the dark shadows under his eyes and receding hairline. The driver looked like an everyman. You would not remember him if he murdered your family and left a painted portrait of himself in your living room.

He said to The Killer, "Your Night Ride, sir. Get in." His voice was a syrupy Russian croak. Friendly like a firing squad told to wrap their fingers around the triggers and keep shooting until the prisoner was nothing more than a bullet-riddled meat bag hanging from a pole.

That rattled The Killer somewhat. In his business, being kept in the dark is like being blindfolded and told to perform a balancing act on a hire wire above the city. He knew the driver could be anybody. *Anybody.* On the driver's lap right now could be a loaded semiautomatic with armor-piercing rounds ready to rip him to pieces.

But what choice did he have?

So, thinking of the paycheck, The Killer took a long exhale, got in, and let the beast swallow him whole.

The inside of the Mercedes was a planet with no stars. All the windows tinted black and the back seat long and hard like a basketball bench, but covered in the finest black Italian leather. *And it'd be a shame to ruin the color with brain matter*, he instinctively thought out of nowhere. But that was the way The Killer's mind worked. The car was perfect for a secret business meeting but a private execution too. No doubt people had been strangled, gouged, or shot up in here before. He knew the car was bulletproof, but he wondered if the interior cradled sound as well. Probably.

"Nice ride," The Killer said.

"Hmm, yes. Our employer knows how to travel in style," Mr. Driver said without looking back.

Our employer. The Killer thought that sounded odd. "And who's that?" he asked. "I mean—I'm here, aren't I? About time I got the full briefing, don't you think?"

A long moment of silence followed the question.

The driver finally said, "I'm not at liberty to say. I only drive the car, sir."

"Fine. At least tell me where we're headed. I'm getting fidgety back here."

"Plyos. Our employer has a house there."

The Killer quickly went through the Russian Rolodex in his brain. He knew about the town from his studies. Plyos was two hours outside Moscow—a quiet, peaceful village in Privolzhsky District, located off the right bank of the Volga River. There was not much to talk about—no major businesses or celebrities lived there. It was shy, the forgotten stepsister in the Cinderella fairy tale. The last place on Earth anyone would expect to be murdered.

The drive took them out of Moscow toward Plyos, where the main road followed the valleys and river and hunting trails lined with potholes. Neither one of them spoke another word to each other for two hours. The only noise came from a tire meeting a pothole: *pop, bounce.*

Two hours later, now well and truly out of the city and in the heartland of the lush green countryside of Plyos, Mr. Driver brought the Mercedes to a halt, right next to a fat tin mailbox slathered in black paint. On one side of the mailbox was the name ALEXANDER.

From the back seat window, The Killer spotted an old English-style manor up ahead, well past the mailbox. The multifloored manor looked like something that belonged in the board game *Clue*. Large sunflower bushes leaned up against it.

A person's home says everything you need to know about them without saying anything at all. Homes are a psychological snapshot, a map to the stars of someone's thoughts. The way someone chooses to decorate the walls, the halls, the kitchen, even the bathroom. For example, are the rooms uplifted by bright, burning colors or draped in black? And what is the state of each room? Organized, or messy like a war-torn battlefield? This says a lot about someone's state of mind.

The driver turned the car off, letting the low rattle hum on the hot engine hiss and moan.
"We're here," he purred, his words drifting through the cabin air like an uncomfortable hazy mist.

The Killer did not know what to say. So he repositioned the pistol in his pants pocket and hopped out of the car. It felt good to finally stretch his limbs, to feel the cool mountain breeze on his skin. To feel alive again.

Then he saw him.

A tall, angular man stood out in front of the manor, watching the car like a bird, or more specifically, a crow ready to feast. The man had faded dyed black hair and leathery skin stretched taut across prominent bones in his face and hands.

The Killer's eyes widened. He'd seen this man before. It took ten seconds for his brain to shuffle through a hundred thousand mug shots stored in his memory bank—but he did find him. Edgar

Alexander, the famous American horror author, familiar from old television commercials and the back covers of dusty paperbacks.

While The Killer had never been much of a devout reader, some people are impossible to hide from. Aside from Stephen King, the last half century of American horror/mystery literature belonged to Edgar Alexander, hands down. Every bookstore, from major chain to mom-and-pop, carried his pen's work.

But the writer was illustrious in his mystery. The Killer tried to recall what he knew about the writer, aside from the books and numerous movie adaptations, but could not come up with anything at all. His personal life was more tightly wrapped than a mummy. For a famous recluse with millions of dollars, it made sense to build a house out here. But what did not make sense was why he'd hired The Killer. Why someone who murdered fictional people with the tip of his pen would want to reenact that in real life.

Edgar Alexander said nothing. He did not have to. The Killer followed him into the house, where the author led the way into a vast hall so dark that a multitude of lamps failed to light it dimly. At the end of the hall was a dining room with a dinner table made for ten men—abandoned. Empty.

But without notice, like a car changing lanes—Edgar pivoted on one heel and cut through another area of the house to the kitchen. The kitchen was gargantuan, covered in ceramic floor tiles with a wood ceiling, and with a round pizza oven, Italy-style with furnace. Various pots and pans slumped from an overhanging rack, and a set of sharp steak knives rested on a counter.

"We'll talk in the library. I always feel the most comfortable beside a book," Edgar said. His voice held a strong midwestern American accent. But unlike most people, when he talked, he did not slow down or interrupt the speed of his step. Instead, he did the polar opposite, propelling himself faster, like a motorboat blade churning river water.

The library was eerie, lit by torture chamber candlelight. At the back of the room was a brown oak desk that looked like it belonged in the Oval Office. Judging by the typhoon of ink-stained papers scattered on top, this was Edgar's bestseller portal. It was the factory that churned out this century's greatest works.

On the wall above the oak desk was a family portrait. Edgar and his wife, a beautiful woman with bourbon-colored hair, and their son, who looked a lot like prepubescent Haley Joel Osment from *The Sixth Sense*, smiled down on The Killer, their ghostly white grins dancing in the eternal orange candlelight.

Edgar's family obviously wasn't here now. No woman's or child's voices filled the empty halls or rooms. The Killer guessed Edgar had probably sent them away for the day, maybe to the Moscow markets or mall for a fun movie/ice cream excursion. Anything to hide them from evil as best he could…

To The Killer's right was a gigantic bookshelf packed with hardcovers. The bookshelf stretched the whole length of the room. If someone picked a tale off the shelf and started reading, it might take them years to shuffle through its brothers and sisters. Some of the titles he recognized. Edgar had specific tastes: Agatha Christie, Dorothy Sayers, Edgar Allen, Lovecraft, Bradbury, Ellison, King, Straub. All of his competition for best thriller writer of all time.

Edgar Alexander gave a crocodile smile. In the orange candlelight, he looked imposing. Exactly like Dracula hanging upside down from a ceiling beam. Waiting to strike. The author looked better in person than the black-and-white dust jacket photo on the back covers of his books. Up close, he was a striking man with pointy shoulders and large black baby doll eyes. If you looked long enough into them, you might find yourself sinking in like a black tar pit from the Jurassic age.

Edgar trotted toward The Killer, extending his hand. The grip was firm, no doubt strengthened by decades pounding away at a keyboard. "Thank you for coming all the way out here. My name is Edgar Alexander—"

But The Killer cut him off. "I know who you are. I don't read that much, Mr. Alexander, but I've heard of you. Your reputation precedes itself."

"Well, coming from you—someone who lives what I write—that might be the biggest compliment of my career." The horror author grinned from ear to ear.

But the Killer did not blink. He was not into stroking anyone's ego; he only talked in facts. "I have to be honest—I had no idea any famous American lived out here."

Edgar nodded. "No one does. I moved out here ten years ago for that very reason and have not looked back. When I was a boy, there was always talk of thermonuclear war with the States. Every good story needs an antagonist, you see, and Soviet Russia was ours. People feared the Russians because our leaders, the system, told them to. My whole life, I fought the system. Do you know how many people in the beginning of my career demanded that I quit? They told me I was wasting my life writing silly stories. That I wouldn't sell squat—or that I was another hack. An ape with a ink pen. Well, I eventually showed them all. Every single last one of them. And now I live here—behind enemy lines?" Edgar curled his lips into a sly sneer. "Showing them all once and forever."

"Cute. And very compelling Mr. Alexander. But you flew me out here to complete a job. It's time you tell me what exactly that is, so I can get paid. Those are the rules I play by."

The Killer did not take his eyes off the author. He studied the wordsmith up and down like a body scanner, taking in every ridge and line on his aging skin. They both studied people for a living, though one did it for more nefarious purposes. But the duo were more alike than different. Both intelligent, purpose-driven men.

“I wouldn’t refer to my life’s work as ‘cute,’ but you are correct. Far too much talking on my part.” Edgar narrowed his eyes. “Time for business.”

Edgar Alexander walked over to a lonely spot on the bookshelf; he took a couple hardbacks off the shelf and set them in a neat stack on the carpet floor, smiling to himself as he did so.

Hidden behind the books was a matte-black attaché case, worth around a thousand dollars, with twin Cagiva combination barrel locks and pigskin suede lining. Edgar took the attaché case and handed it to The Killer.

“There’s seventy-five thousand dollars in there. Or, one half of the payment for coming out here under such…shall we say, mysterious circumstances. What do they call it in your field? A Night Ride? Anyway, I’m a prominent figure in the entertainment industry, so me being caught canoodling with someone of your caliber wouldn’t end well for me. The secrecy was necessary.” When Edgar spoke, he did so chin up, with an authoritarian status.

But The Killer saw through it. “I understand that part, Mr. Alexander. But what about my other half?”

“When the job’s complete. I have to know you won’t run out on me.”

“Or you mean, murder you and run out.” The Killer’s words sliced through the air like samurai swords.

“Sure. I write about men like you all the time but have never actually dealt with one before.” Edgar tapped his foot. A soft, nervous pitter-patter, the only sound in the library.

Right then and there, The Killer knew who, psychologically, was in charge now. One of them was just having a weird day, while the other was a civilian ejecting himself into outer space. Totally unaware. And scared. This made The Killer grin on the inside.

"Mm. Okay, Mr. Alexander, despite the theatrics, I do believe you. Now tell me about the job—and also why you went out of your way to hire me when there are hundreds, if not thousands, of equally qualified Russian hit men and gangsters that would probably do the job for half the price. Hiring me seems like a lot of hassle. Wouldn't you agree?"

But Edgar Alexander did not reply. His eyes were hooked on the attaché case instead.
"Wait, hold on. You won't count it? To make sure all the money is there."

This elicited a chuckle from The Killer. "Oh no, Mr. Alexander. If I find out that you shorted me, I'll come back here and shove one of your bestsellers down your throat. You'll die very slowly and painfully," he replied calmly. Not a single other thought went through The Killer's mind when he said this.

The stupid, smug look on the author's face—the one he'd perfected over years of staying at the top, of being loved, adored, and worshipped by millions—was long gone. He could exile himself all the way out here, but the human element never left. Edgar was just another man. Albeit scared shitless and in over his head. But The Killer had taken out a thousand of them before.

"Are you always this charming?" Edgar croaked, his voice a scratchy record.

"Only on the first date, Mr. Edgar. Now come to it. Why me, and what's the job?"

"Well"—Edgar exhaled—"the reason I hired you specifically is because you're American. And despite the differences I have with my home country, people there know how to tell a good story, don't they? Hollywood and New York City are the land of dreams for many people around the globe. Every year, thousands of them travel to kick-start their career in show biz. They all believe what they want to believe. And there is nothing more American than that."

"I'm lost, Mr. Alexander. Explain yourself."

"I hired an American because I know Americans appreciate a good horror story. And I have one for you right now. There's a monster living in my son's bedroom closet.

"I need you to kill it."

Here There Be Monsters

The Killer didn't say a word. Instead, he reached for the pistol in his pocket and pulled it out. Quick like a close shave.

"Are you high, Edgar? Been sniffing your ink pens?" he asked while aiming the weapon at the writer's gut.

Edgar's eyeballs became fat goose eggs when he saw the gun. Terribly frightened—slithering-snakes-in-a-basket anxiety. "No! Don't point that thing at me."

"You're the one playing children's games with a hired gun, Edgar."

"This is no game. The money's real!" Now everything the author had pretended to be was gone. In a million people's minds around the globe, Edgar Alexander was the epitome of horror. A dark lord wielding a bloody pen. But now…nothing.

The Killer felt pity for what he saw in the man's eyes. He knew Edgar wasn't drugged up, just delusional. A shell of his former self. "Get me the other seventy-five thousand now, and I'll be on my way. If not, I'll splatter your brains on the bookcase. Then watch your maid scrub you up with a sponge."

"Just listen to me, goddammit!" Edgar said, dried spittle stuck to his pink worm lips.

The Killer swerved the pistol one inch and pulled the trigger, shooting right past the author's hip. A stack of papers on the desk exploded. Hot smoke followed by a loud firework boom. Edgar fell over onto his back, screaming.

"I'm not fucking around, Mr. Alexander. Give me my other half. Now."

"Christ! AHH! Put it down, please. Please!" Edgar hollered. He sat on the floor now, with both hands shielding his face. If the author was ten years older, he might've had a heart attack. "Just listen to me—"

"Enough! I'm counting to three, Mr. Alexander. Then I'm going to assume you're short, and I'll have no choice but to blow a hole through you as compensation."

"Please! Hear me ou—"

"One."

"This wasn't a trick! I knew very well who I hired and for what purpose."

"Two."

Edgar's face morphed into some silly grey putty. A half-dead awakened zombie seeing sunshine for the very first time. Aware.

"Okay! Okay! The other half is in the safe behind my desk. But I have to get up to go get it! Don't shoot me."

"Good." The Killer lowered the gun. No expression on his face whatsoever. "Now hurry up."

And on cue, Edgar scrambled to his feet and ran somewhat lopsidedly to the desk, his loafers making scraping noises on the carpet.

"It better all be there, for your sake." The Killer exhaled, watching the author squat down behind the desk and do some fast adjustments. The sound of a lock spinning.

Click. Click. Click. Poof.

"Easy, Edgar. Don't come up too quick now, or I'll assume you're holding a loaded weapon."

But he wasn't. Ten seconds later, Edgar began stacking green stacks on the top of the desk. Going back and forth under the table like a factory machine. When he was done, he was out of breath. He wiped away a bead of sweat trickling down his forehead. "There you go. See?"

"I do. Now pack it up in another case, and I'll be on my way, Mr. Alexander. Your driver better be waiting for me out front."

"He should be. I instructed him to wait however long." Edgar raised both hands above his head.

"You can put your hands down. I'm not going to shoot you, even though you deserve it," The Killer said. Knowing all too well the author had played into his bluff.

The truth was…he wouldn't have shot Edgar even if he didn't have the money. Maybe punish him with a bullet to the hip or arm, but no kill shot. Edgar Alexander was too high profile. Offing celebrities always brought the wrong type of attention anyway.

But Edgar didn't see it that way; he'd only stared into the barrel of the gun and seen his life flash before his eyes. Because he was a civilian and The Killer wasn't.

Edgar said, "You have the money. Now, give me sixty seconds to change your mind."

"About what? More stories of monsters? If I wanted to hear those, I would have read your books instead."

"Sixty seconds…"

"Thirty. Go."

A rush of endorphins sailed through Edgar's pale, frail frame, straightening him up like a flag pole. "Monsters are very real and exist in and outside of fiction, as much as you'd like to disbelieve it. There are two types of monsters. People like…yourself. And the other are the unexplainable, fantastical beasts that occupy our nightmares and dark spaces. I figure the only way to win is to pit one against the other. To fight fire with fire, so to speak."

"I think you've said just about enough, Mr. Alexander."

"Then another hundred thousand should change your mind. I'm a very wealthy man—a quarter million is nothing to me."

"For doing what?" The Killer tightened his grip on the pistol butt. He ached to cock it back and shoot—but he couldn't because of the repercussions.

"Another hundred thousand to walk over to my son's room and take a look for yourself. Surely that has to be the simplest offer ever thrown your way. Why, you'd be a fool not to take my money."

"You're a very sick man, Mr. Alexander. And one day, you're going to get your family hurt because of it."

"Oh, you saw my family's picture on the wall, did you? That's my wife, Katherine, and my boy, Dean. They're dead now."

When Edgar spoke their names, a chill thrust itself through the air. Haunting the room.

"You murdered them, Edgar."

"No, the thing upstairs did. It ate them. First my son and then my wife. And eventually my whole staff too. The cook, the maids, an electrician, and one homeless man I scooped up from the streets of Moscow. I thought offering a sacrifice might make it go away, but no. Nothing's worked. So now you're my only solution."

The Killer didn't blink. Not once. "Edgar, listen to me very carefully. I said I wouldn't shoot you before, but now I'm thinking I might out of principle. So shut up. Pack my other seventy-five. And call the driver—*now*."

"Fine. Two hundred thousand on top of the one-fifty you already have. I don't have that in cash, but you can watch me wire it to whatever account you choose," Edgar slurred. A single bead of sweat slid down his knuckles.

"You're out of your mind if you expect me to believe your boogeyman story."

"You don't have to. All I'm paying you to do is go look for yourself..."

The Killer lowered the gun—and time seemed to stop. Frozen in midair like an eagle.

"I want two-fifty. That on top of the one-fifty you already owe me. I'll listen to any campfire story you have on deck. But when all this nonsense is over, Edgar, you never contact me again, or I'll kill you."

Edgar licked the dried sweat off his lips.

"Done."

The Storytellers

The Killer didn't remember much about his childhood. Or if he'd had one at all.

People will tell you that they have fond memories of summer play. Ice cream trucks. Friends skipping rope and shooting hoops. Trading baseball cards. Crushing on the girl next door. You know, kid shit.

He had none of that. Anything The Killer tried to recall before he was eighteen had been wiped out. Expunged by bullets, knives, grenades, garrote wire, and death.

Death he was responsible for.

Some days, he spent hours searching for the memories of boyhood. Searching for a purpose and meaning away from the gun trigger or knife handle. But that was like mining for gold in Arizona. Hopeless.

Although The Killer would never admit it to anyone, he didn't think he was human at all. Deep down, in the black tar pit of his heart, he believed he was an alien. An extraterrestrial sent from somewhere far away to kill human beings. Maybe from the Creator himself? Who really knew?

The Killer didn't believe he was simply a psychopath, even though a bunch of textbooks written by some very intelligent human beings said so. He felt. And felt hard. Topics like poverty and famine bothered him deeply, as did the fact that some people lived like kings while others suffered immeasurably just a few miles away.

Humanity was always destined to devour itself like a snake chomping on its own tail. The Killer just helped speed up the process.

Victor Mick was one of those types too. Professional, just like The Killer. But louder, more round, and his face a bird's-nest beard with a pair of tiny needle-drop black eyeballs peeking out above them.

By all accounts, Mick was The Killer's only "friend." None of the gunmen kept the same number for long, though, so chances of them communicating regularly were slim to none. But if The Killer knew Mick was in the same area, either completing a contract or on vacation, the men met up and talked about anything but work.

Mick's nickname in the industry was "Dummy" because of the method in which he killed people. With his car.

No guns (he didn't own one), knives, explosives, or toothbrushes. Unlike The Killer, Mick only took jobs that suited his style of killing. No office floor sniper scoping or garroting from behind a shower curtain, only head-on car collisions. He was addicted to the pungent smell of oil, crumpled metal, and broken bones.

Mick liked to track the hit for weeks and follow the targets to their daily schedules. Like knowing what kind of car they drove or were driven in. Which shortcuts they took to get to work. And how fast they or their driver drove, and did the driver obey the laws or run through every stoplight on the way.

Mick spent fifty thousand a year on old cars, beat-up relics like Ford Mustangs and GTs. His only connection was a car dealer named Grady in west Indiana. Mick would buy the car from Grady ahead of time and spend thousands of dollars making it crash proof. Padded door frames, no-snap seat buckles that couldn't be even cut with a hunting knife, inflatable air bags with extra cushion, and a tin cage wall (blowtorch fused) to stop Mick's body from flying through the windshield or being cut to bits by glass upon impact.

When he ran them head on.

After the collision, Mick, who was always “a little” banged up, with a few cuts, scratches, or possible bruising here or there, but never anything serious, would then crawl out of the car window and step onto a battlefield.

Getting hit head on by another car at seventy miles an hour isn’t pretty, though. Sometimes the target’s driver (if they had one) lived through the crash. Other times not.

But Mick’s target, who was in the back seat with no air bag or seatbelt, never lived. Always there was something like a broken neck, or exploded spleen, or crushed vertebra. Fatal injuries like that. Victor Mick wasn’t a doctor by any means, but knew a dead fish from a flopping one, and that’s all that mattered.

The cars Mick used had no plates or identification whatsoever. All someone investigating would ever wonder was why one car was driverless and padded to the gills with crash test safety precautions that rivaled Formula 1.

Not that anyone asking questions mattered, though. Because by the time they did, Mick was long gone—in some cases, already on to the next job. Back to the dealership. To Grady. And back to crash test dummy–proofing his next murder weapon.

The Killer never once asked Victor “Dummy” Mick why he was obsessed with cars—or why he only killed that way. Because he himself couldn’t remember either.

No memories of childhood, adolescence, or any family either. Just one big black hole—an unwrapped Christmas present with nothing inside but the aroma of diesel fluid and blood, which always tasted like copper when a finger dipped and licked.

Maybe that’s why the two men became so close. Admittedly, The Killer had never had a friend in his life. No one to shake hands with outside of the trigger on his rifle.

"You should write more, my friend. Men like you and I are wolves. And wolves can't be taught anything," Mick said one day over a glass of warm milk.

The duo happened to be between jobs in Mexico City at the same time and had decided to reunite at a local bar. The bar itself was a shamble shack with no name but had cheap beer, tiled floor, and prostitutes willing to do anything for forty dollars. Not to mention the rats scurrying about the kitchen floor like lit fireworks. But no one in the bar cared—or noticed. The locals were too coked up or smashed to worry.

Which was perfect.

Because no one admired the two foreign-looking gentlemen at the end of the bar ordering glasses of warm milk. If the men did get a look or two though, it was a quick smirk accompanied by a homosexual slur uttered under soft breath by those who didn't know the only reason the hitmen despised alcohol was because it impaired the senses and flattened focus. Which are crucial elements in staying alive.

Or, funnily enough—that the milk sippers were even hitmen. And possibly the most dangerous men in the city, let alone the bar.

The moment the milk met Mick's lips and he couldn't talk, The Killer wanted to talk about his day. The one spent curled up in a motel bathroom with a knife to his neck, thinking about cutting the alien chip out of his head.

But he didn't, because Mick was the only man on the planet he listened to, and Mick had the floor.

When Mick put the glass back down on the bar napkin, he leaned in close so The Killer could smell his breath. "Compadre, I told you to write more. But I'm getting the feeling you've never written at all."

“No, Mick, I haven’t. But write about what?” The Killer replied, watching Mick guzzle the last bit of milk down and then wipe a white, creamy mustache off his face.

“Your past. Ever heard the saying, *the things we think become our reality*? Well, I took that to heart and penned my own story. In it, I had a family once, but before all of this. There were four of us. My wife, Dolly, and our two kids, Theo and Harper. I devoted a whole chapter of my story to them. Rewrote it three whole times too.”

“Sounds fun, but I’m not much of a writer.”

“But you are curious.” Mick grinned. “I know that, because I have a name, and you don’t.”

The Killer only thought about the aliens again. He circled the top of his milk glass with a lonely finger. “We play God for a living but only know the names of the men we’ve killed. Maybe that’s the way it’s supposed to be, Victor. Stop writing your stories,” The Killer replied, getting up to pay the bar tab and go.

Slipping away into the dark night—a nothingness he knew all too well. Guided only by an alien radio transmission signal in his head and the pistol in his pocket…

While, halfway around the world, Edgar Alexander contemplated placing a nickel-plated Beretta under his chin and ending it. *It’d be so easy, like slipping into a nice warm bath. One little flick of your finger and every pain would be gone*, his mind chimed, driven solely by spikes of paranoia and fear. And disgust. Hatred.

Upstairs, the thing was making noises again. Creaking. Cracking. Growling. Moaning.

For the last month, the beast had wanted his utmost attention, but Edgar wouldn’t give in. Like most of life’s problems.

That didn't mean he wasn't in any pain.

Nothing he'd written about compared to the horror of handing his son to the beast to be skewered and devoured alive. Meat and gristle torn from flesh, sinewy limbs popped off like doll parts. Edgar had thought a sacrifice might drive it away, but it didn't.

So he tried his wife next. Knocking her out with an ammonia rag and zip-tying her to a wheelchair. But that didn't work either.

The beast took her too and asked for more. Just like Edgar's appetite for flushing a story out, it couldn't get enough.

Every housekeeper went without a fight. And the kitchen cook and gardener too. All funneled through the same meat grinder.

Edgar didn't intend to budge. Wherever the thing had come from, it could find its way back. Outer space, a jungle, or…

My own mind. Edgar laughed to himself. Listening to another flurry of scratches coming from upstairs. Knowing all too well the beast was stuck like glue. To stop it from coming downstairs, he'd boarded up the stairwell with tin metal sheets using hammer spikes. Confining the beast to the upstairs hall and guest bedrooms.

For now.

"Sir, you wanted to see me."

Edgar squinted, the rims of his eyes red from little sleep, spying Emilio, his driver, who stood near the door, arms clasped by his sides, chin tilted up. At attention.

Emilio was a good man and even better employee. Loyal. Trustful. Being born and raised in the slums of Moscow with not much of a future, he'd been fortunate to be taken in by the wealthy writer.

And Emilio knew it too. It wasn't rocket science to figure out what was going on. Like why, except for Emilio, virtually all the staff had been let go recently. Fired like shotguns.

The truth was…

What Edgar was really doing was getting rid of dead weight, restaffing the house with harder-working grunts like Emilio. And the thought made Emilio grin on the inside like a schoolboy, simply because he'd survived. Proved his worth where the others didn't.

And Emilio was damn proud of that.

"Ah yes, Emilio, you found the American for me?"

"Yes, sir, Mr. Alexander. My contact is talking to his representation now. We should have an answer by Tuesday."

"That's in three days, Emilio."

"The American's representation informed me he's on a job in Mexico City at the moment, sir."

"Hmm. Well, we'll pay him real good money to come out here. Double—no, triple his usual fare. Tell them that as soon as you leave this room. Understood, Emilio?"

"Yes, sir. Although, I can get you someone cheaper. A local—a friend of my father's."

"No! Strictly an American, Emilio. Understand?"

Emilio spied the Beretta pistol lying on top of his boss's desk. The weapon stuck out like an ugly child disillusioned by their place in society. But Emilio didn't waver. He'd been around guns and the types of men who used them his whole life. His own father, a former Russian mob enforcer (and Emilio's contact to the underworld), had been murdered by one. Shot dead in the street in front of their house by a rival gang member when Emilio was only six years old.

Emilio knew real pain and unbelievable terror. But also, because of the wealthy scribbler before him, love and respect. And so *whatever* Edgar needed, Emilio was there for him. Including using his father's past mob ties to find a hired gun for services rendered.

No questions asked.

Even though he personally didn't believe his employer was a killer, or ever imagined killing someone (well, outside of one of his horror fiction stories). Like actually putting a bullet in someone's brain and then going about his day.

Because of his upbringing, Emilio knew that not just anyone was capable of performing the task, even if their own lives depended on pulling the trigger. Morals and conscience have a way of haunting the most hardened men like ghosts. Ripping away at their souls until nothing is left.

"I understand, sir. By tomorrow morning, everything will be sorted out."

"Good. Emilio, you know my wife and son are…on vacation right now."

"In the Maldives, sir, yes. You told me already. Sounds amazing."

"Well, obviously, I'd like this all behind me before they get back. So get this right."
Edgar's tone was hollow and unapologetic.

"Understood."

"Great. Oh and by the way, Emilio, I meant to bring this up earlier. You're looking thin these days. Have you lost some weight?"

The obscure question rocked Emilio back a little. "Um…not that I'm aware of, sir. Why?"

"A hungry tiger would spit you back out. Nothing but rags on top of bone. If I increase your salary by fifteen percent, which is beyond generous, I expect you to put on fifteen pounds. Can you do that for me?"

Could he do that for Edgar? Of course he could. He'd do anything for the man. "Yes, I can, sir, but may I ask why?"

"Just in case, Emilio. That's why…just in case. Now go!" Edgar Alexander shouted, causing a very confused Emilio to nod quickly and walk out the library door, enveloping the room in a thickening mist of silence again.

When Emilio had gone, Edgar sat back down and exhaled, running his fingers through his greying hair but not once taking an eye off the Beretta, the *boom-bap* of his heart thumping in his chest like a bomb. "Yes…just in case I need another sacrifice, my friend," Edgar muttered to himself.

Just waiting again.

Waiting for the amusement park upstairs to reopen. Which it did, a whole agonizing ten seconds later—the familiar scratching, the clawing, the hard thumps all coming to life.

Followed by the ever-present screams of his wife's face being ripped off. Screams only he could hear.

Over and over and over again.

Midnight Looks Good on You

Edgar and The Killer (with machine pistol hanging off his shoulder and hunting knife strapped to his thigh) spent the better part of the afternoon wrenching away the metal sheet barrier that blocked off the upper levels of the house. The barrier Edgar had built to keep his beast at bay. When they were done, there was sweat pouring down their backs and faces.

"Well, if this didn't wake your monster up, I don't know what will," The Killer spat, pointing the pistol at Edgar's chest.

"Why are you pointing that at me?"

"Because I'm done playing your game, Edgar. You're going up there with me."

"That wasn't part of the deal! I'm paying *you*, remember? Not the other way around."

"How do I know you didn't booby-trap the hallway? Or do something else stupid?"

"For what? To trap you? What do I gain by that?" Edgar snorted.

"I have no clue, Edgar. And frankly, I don't care. Not yet, anyway. But you want to know what I really think? Huh, do you?"

Edgar didn't say a word.

"I think that if I took a shovel and started digging around your backyard, I might find something. A couple hours if I got lucky, a day maybe, two, three tops. I'd find the bodies of the wife and child you murdered. Both of them stacked together naked and neatly like flapjacks, giving the worms something to chew on. Thanks what I think, pal."

The Killer used all his weight to shove the writer up against the staircase wall. Finishing his rant: "Now listen here, sick fuck. You go first, and I'll follow with my pistol pressed against your back. If you make *any* movement I don't like, I'm putting a bullet in you."

Edgar only nodded, giving The Killer a shaky yes.

"Good. Now up we go. Start walking."

The second story of Edgar Alexander's home was a single hallway bathed in a distillery of greys and purples. With shiny slivers of sunlight peeping out through a duo of barred windows on opposite ends of the hallway, the ambiance was deader than a graveyard at midnight.

The moment Edgar stepped foot in the hall, his face melted to a icicle pop white and his knees began to tremble. Panic coursed through his body and played video games of paranoia with his brain.

Even The Killer saw it, watched him gasp for air and drop down on one knee. "Get up, Edgar. Stop playing around."

"Fuck you," Edgar spat, somehow making it back to his feet. Eyes closed. Focused.

"So where's this thing at? I don't see it."

"Either sleeping… or waiting on me to bring it more food."

"Oh for Christ's sake. You really are one in a million. I can see how you've sold all those books now," The Killer grumbled, moving the pistol off the writer's back. He had a feeling he didn't need it anymore. The circus was about ove—

Until Edgar flung himself against a wall, arms and legs plastered together like a mouse caught in a trap. "Shhh. I just heard it. In my boy's bedroom, just like I told you before. Down there!"

His finger flicked sideways, pointing down toward the last door at the end of the hall. From what The Killer could see, it was a peach-and-cream door with several markings on it. Markings that looked like knife stabs…or something along the line of it.

"Didn't you hear me?" said Edgar.

"Yeah, I remember you telling me that, but calm down. I can't have you all over the place right now," The Killer said, poking the pistol back into Edgar's spine. "Walk me to the door, and no funny business."

"I-I can't," Edgar stuttered.

"I'll twist the knob and check the room out, but I'm not walking down there by myself."

"F-fine. But if…if it comes out, you better shoot it. You understand?"

"Sure, whatever you say, boss." The Killer nudged him, edging the two of them down the hall toward the room. Ever so slowly. Achingly slowly, actually.

Then, something happened.

As they drew closer to the door, The Killer's head started to hurt. Not too painfully. Just a little thump where he knew the microchip was. He stopped and applied a hard thumb on the sore spot. Massaging it ever so gently.

"What's the matter? Why'd you stop?" Edgar said without turning around.

"Nothing. Keep going."

But it was something. Little green specks in the corner of each eye now. Flashes of light that bopped back and forth. *They're trying to tell me something*, The Killer thought to himself, looking down at the gun in his hand and the boots on his feet. And then at Edgar Alexander and the ridiculous situation they were in.

Of course there was no beast. No monster of the manor. They were a bunch of grown men playing children's games. This was no different than Commando, or G.I. Joe, or Cowboys and Indians, however you wanted to look at it.

The Killer felt like a boy now. Not actually himself, but a long-lost prototype from a forgotten childhood. Imagining the pistol in his palm was a water gun seemed a lot more fun.

And he smiled. For the first time in years. Feeling invigorated again.

Right as Edgar pivoted round, and clasped the ammonia rag—he one he'd kept stuffed inside his pocket all along— over The Killer's face.

And even though The Killer went for his pistol, it was far too late. All the life drained out of his arms, legs, and chest and a weakness he'd never known took over. A slumber deeper than the dead.

And he was out.

***

Bedrooms are sanctuaries. Portals for people to slip out of their human suits and into something more comfortable.

A child's bedroom is no different. While children's lives are less complex, they still require more time to develop their own personalities. To write their own stories.

Dean Alexander hadn't quite done that before he died.

When The Killer woke up, he was naked from head to toe and bound to one of Edgar's dinner table chairs by electrical wire and duct tape.

Stuck.

But taped to his right hand was an old plastic walkie-talkie. One that clearly worked, judging by the green light flashing on top.

His head hurt and the world felt like it was doing the breaststroke through a fishbowl. Nauseated—but alive nevertheless.

"Fuck—I'm going to rip your head off, Edgar," he growled. He hoped that if he shut both eyes, the spinning would cease. And when it did, he opened his eyes and was able to take a long look around and pick out more of his surroundings.

He was in Dean Alexander's abandoned bedroom, and the door had been bolted shut. And even though the window curtain, a slim purple cape, was closed, he could just make out the silver moon winking at him through it.

It was night now, which meant he must've been unconscious for hours. At least three to four, depending on the time.

Dean Alexander's bedroom had seen better days, though. Now it looked more Ted Bundy than Toys"R"Us, being covered in filth, dust, and cobwebs.

The boy's bed, which was shaped like a race car, had been completely stripped, except for the rusty iron torture rack bed frame underneath. A skeleton without a spirit. And there was nothing on the walls either: no elementary school drawings, posters, toys, or sports medals anywhere. No sign whatsoever that a normal boy ever once lived here. For all intents and purposes, Edgar had morphed his child's bedroom into a prison cell.

The Killer looked up and saw the bedroom closet with the rubber band looped round both door handles. The closet was no bigger than any normal coat hanger space you'd find in any home. Nothing unusual about it, really—that is, if you disregarded the makeshift band lock.

The walkie-talkie taped to his hand gargled, and he clicked the PUSH button.

"Hey, can you hear me?" chimed a familiar albeit scratchy voice.

"You're a dead man, Edgar Alexander. I hope you know that."

"I don't think you're in any position to talk. Not anymore."

"Then how do you see it, Edgar? Tell me where this story goes. You're the writer."

"I already told you the ending, but you weren't listening. Remember I said it was waiting on me—to bring it food. That's you. You're the midnight snack."

The Killer snorted. He started doing anything he could to try to free himself from the electrical wire, but couldn't. It was useless. The bastard actually had him. "Cut the shit, Edgar. You hired me to fight it, but now all of a sudden you're feeding me to it. What part of a flip-flop plot hole is that?"

"I flip-flopped because I decided to offer the beast something rare. There aren't many men like you."

"I'm flattered. But what if this thing doesn't like me?"

A sharp radio silence followed for ten seconds that seemed to drag on forever.

"Well, there's always my driver," Edgar said. And then a click.

And he was gone.

Time ticked on like molasses. Although The Killer didn't know the exact time, which was nine o'clock, he could have taken a good ballpark guess. Every thirty minutes or so, Edgar would call in. Just to, in his words, make sure The Killer was "still alive and breathing."

Whatever that meant.

The Killer wasn't going anywhere. But he also knew the midnight hour Edgar dreaded would pass peacefully, like ships in the night, and he'd still be strapped to the stupid chair. Looking naked and dumb as ever.

But then what?

If Edgar had truly played this game with others before, what happened after midnight?

Maybe he comes in and kills them and blocks it out, The Killer thought, imagining a psychosis-inflicted Edgar Alexander breaking down the bedroom door at 12:01 and jamming a knife into his chest. Or, even worse, storming in and shooting The Killer in the head with his own pistol, and then waking up in the morning and blaming it all on the monster.

All certain possibilities that led one way. Death.

Two hours later, around eleven thirty, The Killer decided to clear his mind, going through a familiar memory exercise to slow his heart rate down and give him more room to think clearly. In his head, he imagined he was cleaning his gun. Taking it apart and wiping it down, step by step.

First, he jacked the slide and pulled it toward himself. Then, he tilted it sideways to get a healthy look at the chamber. Checking the bullets was a must. He also imagined racking them out and collecting them in his palm like AA tokens after a meeting. Repeating the process over and over in his head helped him feel calm again. And in control of his own mind.

Or so he thought.

Because, ten minutes later, the walkie-talkie cackled in The Killer's taped hand. A harsh, eerie static. Unlistenable. And distant. As if someone—or something—had jammed the signal.

"Edgar? Edgar!" The Killer growled, holding the button down. Click. Click. Nothing but muffled scratches.

As the bedroom closet slowly opened…

Birthing a black void deeper than the eye could see. No swinging coats on hooks or shoes piled up against a back wall. In fact, there was no back wall at all, only a tunnel leading into absolute darkness.

"Okay, Edgar—funny. I don't know how you did that, but it worked. You really are the master of suspense! " he chortled. Thumping the walkie-talkie again.

A stench of foul meat drifted out of the void and permeated the room in waves, making The Killer gag. His face flushed gooey green, nose runny, eyes irritated red.

"Dammit, Edgar, what's going on!" he hacked, banging the walkie-talkie against his thigh. "EDGAR!!"

While something in the dark stirred. Hungry.

***

Downstairs, Edgar Alexander held The Killer's gun in one hand and his Beretta in the other. Making sure both were loaded and the safety cocked off. And although he admired the weapons like art, he knew that they were well and truly no match for whatever lurked in the dark.

The clock on the library wall read exactly two minutes after midnight. A hundred and twenty seconds after the walkie-talkies lost contact. But that was normal. For whatever reason, the beast always gorged alone. Finger-licking meat from bone until it had its fill.

Much like how an author pens a book.

At 12:20, Edgar smiled to himself, knowing great work takes great sacrifice.

And began to write.

Dating for the Damned

Dating is just a board game for serial killers. Honestly, take a look at the fucking thing. In what other professional venue is it socially acceptable to meet strangers? The very idea of dating brings a shiver to my spine, the kind of shiver you get watching a scary movie with the lights off.

Women will admit that meeting someone for the first time can be scary. Women want the man with a well-paying job, a good sense of style, a movie star grin, and the ability to talk them down from the edge on a rainy afternoon. The perfect man: the funny guy, well- traveled, well educated, born and raised for one specific purpose in life. For you.

Okay. Now that we've cut through the bullshit with a butter knife, let me take the blindfold off your eyes and remind you that everything that you've been taught is a lie.

The perfect man that you imagined is pure fiction. The dirty little secret is that meeting someone new is much like playing a game of Russian roulette with a loaded pistol pressed against your temple, and my finger is pulling the trigger.

The perfect man is a lie created by attractive men with ulterior motives. We want to meet you, but we need a reason to. I'm *him*. I'm the guy that you ladies hear about on TV or in cheesy romantic comedies. You know—the one starring the guy that you wish was your boyfriend. I'll use this to my advantage.

I'll wear a nice tie, comb my hair, and get a socially acceptable job with benefits and assume my new identity. You were brought up to believe that you deserve a man like me. It's what you were taught as little girls.

However, the well-educated, good-looking, socially acceptable bastards who wouldn't mind seeing what your gall bladder looks like from the inside out are never added into the equation. Is a great-looking man ever considered a threat? The media tells you that a person with sharp cheekbone structure and who owns an expensive car couldn't possibly spend their free time butchering women. Preposterous!

Seriously, weren't good-looking individuals meant for so much more than to turn into mass murderers? Or is that what we want you to believe? If not for my bone structure, who would we know to put on television or incorporate into mass media? To influence the culture of youth, decide when and what to wear, or to run our companies? Who would we pin up on our wall, or declare secular division of worship? Who would you have been taught to trust?

The beautiful woman that sits across from me smiles at the waiter after he stops to refill our glasses of water. I flash him the "fuck off" smile, and he does just that. *You'd lost her for only a minute*, I remind myself while looking into her eyes. Now it was time to play the role that I had been born to play.

If only I could remember her name.

We already had quite a night planned. Later, we would visit the theater, and even later, I would ask her to come home with me so I could show her my surgical kit, which contains my rusty knife used to chisel through flesh and bone. Her name is Janelle, and unbeknownst to her, she is the first "Janelle" that I've ever been with, so I feel like a complete mongrel in slipping up on her name. I'm bored well before our appetizers arrive, twiddling my silver fork on a lone noodle in a bowl of soup, imagining it's my rusty knife playing with her spleen.

I'll tell her I'm thinking about us and gently massage her palm with mine. I'm almost too good; I have to smile, and she smiles back at me. I am pretty fucking spectacular, by the way, in case you were wondering. You have to have a clear topic and well-thought-out ideas and still be able to listen to her when she believes that she has one. But most importantly, what you're saying has to grasp her attention.

Just like this. Never apologize for babbling, and never shrink midstory and let your experiences diminish as you search for the right words. Chew the fucking scenery up. Make extravagant hand gestures and look at her like you're a fucking marine sniper posted low in the tall green grass.

Think of any time you've been to a good film. You have to be the main attraction. Discuss your travel and ambition or how you have grown as a person, and avoid meaningless conversations such as pop culture references, gossip, or whatever you want to call "water cooler" talk. Keep the focus on her.

If she is interested in where you're going in your life, she'll most likely go home with you later tonight. Just like the stranger handing out delicious-looking pink candy to a child from inside an automobile. The venue is jam-packed with handsome stranger faces and a loud assortment of stories from frolicking lips. All around me, I can count them out: at least half a dozen of us seated in the restaurant tonight, and a few recognizable faces that run in the same serial killer circle.

You'll have to be sure to take her to the best spot in town. For our dinner tonight, I began with the Thai appetizer: sliced cucumbers topped with shrimp and hot chili sauce, easy and fun.

Our second course for the evening is the attention grabber. Lobster tail in a *beurre monté*, slowly poached in warm butter with plenty of spice for flavor with a side of small new red potatoes drizzled with truffle oil. Simple and elegant. Do not forget the fresh snow peas and julienned carrots with a refreshing lemon vinaigrette.

For dessert, the flourless chocolate sponge cake served in a martini glass and topped with whipped cream, chocolate ganache, and toasted nuts. Share the spoon. The woman named Janelle excuses herself from the table to use the restroom. I smile and kiss the top of her hand, and Janelle, or whatever the fuck her name is, blushes a drunken raspberry red.

Here's how it goes. Before a meal, you should order a drink such as a martini or a scotch or bourbon highball. These drinks are cold, light, and get the appetite prepared to receive your meal. Also, they provide stellar conversation and help in steering her where you need her to be. Following the meal, you only want to order a dessert drink, such as brandy, cognac, or some liqueur. These actually shut down the taste buds to aid in digestion, thus making her feel the need to use the restroom and allow me to make my most crucial move of the night.

She'll excuse herself and hurry off to the ladies' room, her stiletto heels tapping across the floor like little pins and her tiny arms flinging from side to side. Women either will love their heels or hate them. But sometimes, in Janelle's case, they'll try to alter that to fit a guy's height.

As soon as she turns her back, I reach into my coat pocket for the sleeping pill and pop it into her drink on the table. I can tell that Janelle's starting to appreciate the Rohypnol I gave her toward the end of our dinner. She's slurring her words and saying stupid shit, so I figure that it's time to tip the waiter and be on our way.

One can only imagine what's going through her mind right now—besides the sedative, of course. To be honest, I'd admit to not caring. If my plans go well, her opinion won't matter too much come tomorrow morning. I have to apologize politely to a couple of the tables as we leave the restaurant hand in hand. It's what you do. Take her home as if you'd ordered her for dinner. Get in the cab with her. Be persistent but not intrusive— women like men who will take charge. They like for you to be the man.

She wraps an arm around my neck and kisses me as our yellow cab takes off down the street, spewing exhaust fumes and a particular horror story to go. Then we are home. I turn the key in the keyhole, and we are fumbling with each other's clothing as if we were undergraduate students after a night on the town. I tilt her head back to nibble on her ear, both of them. Janelle mumbles something as her tongue rolls out of her mouth like the red carpet at a Hollywood premiere, and her eyelids roll up into the back of her head.

You'd be surprised how difficult it is to lug a 115-pound human being by each armpit. I push the door open, drag her body inside, and kick the door closed, secluding both of us in my house of horror. Janelle is out cold, so it's easier to snap the handcuffs around her wrists to the bedpost on my bed. Her arms are held high above her head as if she were pleading for mercy, and her legs hang off the side of the mattress, so I have to scoop them back on.

While Janelle is passed out, I get up and go behind the kitchen counter to get the rubber gloves beneath the sink. Once those are on, I begin to lay out a clear blue roll of plastic sheet on the tile floor all around the bedroom. She looks so peaceful over there. I take my shoes off and my belt and then my pants, folding them over the back of the futon, and finally my shirt before moving into the bathroom to step into the shower.

The warm water hits my face and then my bare skin, washing away all of my grime and filth down into the circling drain beneath my feet. It feels good to peel this face off; it's like a Halloween mask that I wear to fit into this society.

This is what all of you women want: something that you had been told to see. Well, don't complain if you don't like what you see underneath. It might frighten you. I turn off the hot water and step out of the shower stall and into the hallway, drying myself off with a black towel that hangs on the handrail of the stall.

Then I drop the towel and strut out into the bedroom, newspaper scrunching beneath my bare feet. Janelle's somehow up and about, although her eyelids are heavy and fat. She's pulling on the handcuffs, twisting her body from right to left. There's drool on her chin like a baby; I wipe the spittle away with my left thumb.

I'm beside her. Close. The carving knife I'd taken from the kitchen is hidden behind my back as if it were a bouquet of flowers for a lover waiting to be presented. A sliver of drool drops down onto her neck, followed by the heat of exhaust of my breath. Struggling half in and half out of reality.

I can hear her heartbeat through her chest like a ticking bomb about to explode. The carving knife in my left hand shouldn't be there, and I can see her coming to this realization. This does not happen to girls like her, but it did. She's thinking, *What did I do? I did everything that I had been told to do.*

The carving knife cuts deep into the inner thigh, and bright blood spills across the sheets and drips down onto the newspaper. I don't even hear her screams, nor do I care. I'm not the same man that she had agreed to go out with tonight. He's long since dead, and she's about to join him.

Dinosaur

The used car lot was filled with dinosaurs. Old dusty pieces of shit no one in their right mind would be caught driving up and down the highway. And one of them was going to be sixteen-year-old Patterson's first car.

The moment the sandy-haired boy and his father pulled into the lot, the boy wanted to disappear like a ghost. Patterson was tall for his age, but flimsy and clunky. And he wasn't especially good looking (even though his mother disagreed), nor was he rocket scientist smart. He was just…average. A "there" kinda kid. Which was okay. Better to be "there" than a loser or stoner or dropout. On the high school social circuit, though, being "there" won't get you laid. Or a date. Or even kissed.

The only thing left was having something other people wanted, whether that be a party house for others to flock to (which wouldn't happen as his parents despised alcohol or any fun whatsoever for that matter) or a nice car. Something shiny and loud with a kick-ass stereo system.

The day before Patterson turned sixteen was the longest twenty-four hours of his life. It seemed to stretch into eons, where centuries of war and chaos reigned supreme in his brain. At that point, all he wanted from life was tomorrow. Because tomorrow he could finally take the driver's test.

Tomorrow came. And so did the test, and so did a passing grade.

But today was different. Gone was the excitement that seemed to burst out of every pore in his body. Now, black dread sailed through a slow-beating heart, one confined by sorrow.

Because what good is having a car if the one you drive looks like something out of *The Road Warrior*?

"Here we are, bud. You excited?" Patterson's father asked as he turned the car off. The keys dangled down like soccer balls in a net.

Patterson sighed. "Dad, these things are dinosaurs. What if they break down on me?"

"Well, that's not going to happen, Pat. We'll pick out a good one for you." His father winked and cracked the driver's-side door open.

Patterson knew that his father knew he was disappointed; it doesn't take a psychic ability to read a teenager's mind. And even though he now sported the middle-aged paunch and horseshoe-shaped hairline, his father had been young once too. A long time ago—but still. He had to remember that driving some hunk of junk through the school parking lot wouldn't improve anyone's reputation.

Patterson wanted to scream. Shout. Cry.

But here they were.

A wobbly fat man stood out front, bobbing up and down with childish glee when they pulled in. The guy looked every bit the cheap salesman, with wire-rimmed glasses, a bushy mustache, a pocket protector, and probably McDonald's wrappers bunched in the trash bin in his office. A loser.

Just like Patterson would be on Monday morning, rolling up in something that belonged in a museum.

"Hey, Rick," said the fat man. "I'm John Morty, we talked over the phone. It's nice to meet you and your son finally." Fat Man Morty came up to shake his father's hand with a mighty grip, hand over palm, squeezing till blood circulation stopped flowing.

Then he turned and extended at hand to Patterson, who shook it halfheartedly.

"You know, I remember my first car. I was sixteen in '86, back when Reagan was president and Springsteen wasn't classic rock. That was a long time ago, but I still remember the excitement the first time I hit the road solo!" Morty chirped, swinging a looped keychain around one stumpy finger as he talked.

"Well, Patterson is really excited. Aren't you, Pat?" Father gave his son an intense stare. One that said, "Play along now, bud."

So Patterson did just that, bobbing his head up and down in approval.

"Good. Well, I've been selling cars for the past twenty years, and you two are in the right place. Nothin' more affordable or safe"—Morty winked at Father—"in this corner of the country."

In the lot behind Morty was a plethora of old cars, most of them looking more like busted-up boxers in the tenth round than automobiles. Chipped paint, scratched windows, low tops, and probably spiders crawling in the trunks.

Patterson looked up at the sky and noticed a string of black clouds rolling over their heads. The clouds were bunched up and looked pissed off—floating bubbles with thunder brewing in their bellies. So, not only was he going home with a hunk of junk, but the world was about to piss all over him too.

Just his luck.

Morty and Father noticed too, because a second later, Fat Man Morty cackled. "Well, oh boy, that wasn't in the forecast."

Father chimed in, "Yeah, weird. Hmm."

"Maybe it's a bad omen," Patterson chirped, sounding younger than he was. Like a little kid in a gladiator ring.

Both of the men yanked their heads back down and laughed. Father slapped him on the shoulder. "Oh come on, Pat. When I was fifteen, I would have shot a horse and bench-pressed it for a car. This is your big day!"

"Yeah, it's big all right," Patterson grumbled, knowing all too well Father would block out his negative attitude.

As he had all day.

They followed John Morty to the back of the lot, which was nothing more than a desolate asteroid with scraps of spaceship and oil cans scattered about. Patterson saw a couple of Chevrolet Silverados, some Chevrolet Camaros, a Dodge Charger, a Toyota Camry, a Honda Accord, and a beat-down Nissan Altima.

And one car with a ghost-white sheet draped over its body, only the wheels visible.

"Alrighty, big man! I have a few cars I think you'll be into. The Toyota Camry is a dog but purrs like a cat. What d'ya think?" John Morty winked and smiled, the yellow stains on his teeth shiny like California gold.

But Patterson thought one thing and one thing only. That no matter what happened in the future, he would never grow up to be like John Morty. He'd rather die. Pointing at Mr. Ghostsheet, he said, "Mmm, maybe. What's that?"

"Oh, that's the neighborhood troublemaker. It's not for sale."

Patterson was walking toward it anyway, seemingly drawn to the pale sheet, stepping out of line with his father and the fat man.

"What type of car is it?" Father asked. Maybe he was a little curious himself.

“A black 1998 Audi. The thing’s actually relatively new compared to a lot of the other cars on the lot, but nobody wants it. I’m selling it for scrap next week.” John Morty huffed, giving his head a rough shake.

“But it runs?”

“Uh, yeah, but it’s not for sale. Like I said.”

“Why? I think I’m interested in this one,” Patterson said out loud. He was circling the Audi like a shark in bloody waters, his eyes laser locked. There was…something about it. But the boy couldn’t quite grasp what.

Now Morty’s car salesman swagger was gone. He looked suspiciously sweaty, and the smell of cheap mall cologne wavered off him. “Because I have to tell you about the car’s history before you buy it. And after I do, you won’t want the thing anymore. No one does.”

Patterson and his father both pivoted and looked right at John Morty, their eyebrows bunched up. Father laughed and said, “Well, damn, I think I’m intrigued too,” like this was all some silly jest.

And in return, Morty sighed, doing his best to remain professional and composed. “Okay, well, the previous owner was killed in it.”

“Whoa. How!” Patterson was unable to stop the question from flying out of his lips like a cannonball.

“He was stabbed. From what I know, it was a carjacking gone wrong.”

“Wow. Yeah, I get why you can’t sell it,” Father muttered, a “holy shit” smirk slapped across his face.

Up above their heads, the dark clouds had clumped together some more, effectively blocking out the sun or anything else cheerful. No doubt, a rainstorm was on the horizon.

"I still want to see it," Patterson replied. He wanted to lift the sheet up like a wet dream of some pretty girl's skirt.

"Pat! You don't want *that* car."

"Why not? Maybe what happened doesn't bother me like it does you," Patterson griped.

"Oh, you're just sixteen, Pat," said his father. "Why on earth would you want this to be your first car? Come on."

"Mr. Morty said it works fine. Isn't that right?" Patterson turned to the salesman, aching for an answer.

"Yes, it runs fine. But listen to your father."

"Nah, don't think I will," Patterson spat, feeling some surge of power—a teenage rebellion—galloping through every limb. He walked up to his father, getting within whispering range, and said, "I want to look at this car. I'm not interested in anything else."

"Pat…no. I'm saying no. Pick something else."

"Then I wanna go home," Patterson replied. Hands on both hips, dead serious.

"Don't be ridiculous."

"I'm not. I just want to see it. I'm not fully into buying the thing yet."

In turn, Father rolled his eyes and gave John Morty a kind of "This is your fault, pal" expression. "Well, Mr. Morty, my son would like to take a look at the car."

"Okay. The keys are in my office. I'll go get them." Morty sighed and waddled off toward his office. A tin brown bell dinged when the door shut behind him.

When Morty came back and handed the keys over to Patterson, he ripped the white tarp off too, bunching it up in a birthday cake–sized ball.

The old car stared back at them like a matador, catching their reflections in the windows. Silent. Still. Unnerved.

But Patterson wasn't afraid. A taste of adventure had camped out on his tongue. Or more so the thrill of being alive and exploring this…graveyard. Through the driver's-side window, he saw a stain on the headrest. Big, fat, beautiful, and bold, a remnant of the crime.

A bloodstain.

Father saw it too; his eyes bugged out. "God! Has the thing been cleaned?"

"Yes, many times. And it was a lot worse before this, believe me." Morty didn't blink.

The keys were already in Pat's shaking hand.

A transfer of power.

"How could you have thought anybody would be interested?" Father asked.

"Because somebody always is. And the car was impounded and likely headed for the crusher. I got it cheap." Morty eyed Father, who watched Pat open the driver's door and slip inside. Adjusting himself.

Above their heads, the black clouds were rumbling now. Bouncing to the beat of their own drum. Anybody else would've guessed it was about to pour down rain.

"Pat, you're not getting this car. So enjoy it while you can, bud," Father exhaled, clearly wishing time would just skip ahead really quickly.

Inside the Audi, Patterson leaned back against the headrest and ignored the goosebumps traveling up and down his arms. He wasn't scared, just…intrigued.

Next, he wrapped both hands around the steering wheel and growled. Pretending he was driving down a dark dirt road at nighttime, the yellow headlights piercing the black like a lance. Searching for…searching for monsters.

"All right, bud, come on out. You've had your fun." Father rapped his knuckles on the glass. His face was expressionless and devoid of any character whatsoever, a soggy wet clay mold of human flesh.

What happened next, though, popped Patterson right out of his daydream.

The driver's seat bucked forward and slammed him headfirst onto the steering wheel. He whacked his nose and smeared blood all over the wheel. Patterson yelped, eyes shut, not able to breathe. Ringing bells were going off in his brain. "What the fuck?" he cackled, reaching for the door handle and wrenching it—to no avail. Neither the handle nor the door itself budged.

Stupid damn thing.

The boy threw his shoulder into the mix, using it to press down on the handle and gritting his teeth. "Come on! Aghh."

***

Outside the Audi, Father and John Morty had backed up a few paces. Shuffling their feet with relative ease.

"How long now?" Father asked, looking down at his watch.

"Oh, it won't be long now. Won't be long at all," Morty replied.

***

Patterson couldn't see out of the windows anymore. The tint had somehow flipped to black—blocking out any view of the outside world.

Embalming him in darkness.

"Hey! Help! Help! Heyyyyy!"

He flung his arms wildly; his sanity slingshot to the farthest corner of the universe and back again.

It was getting hot now. Sweltering. Sweat glistening down his back and neck. Tiny perspiration bombs fell to nuke the floor.

"Dad! Dad! Help! Please!" Patterson moaned, unable to do anything but beg for the nightmare to be over.

When the seat rest prickled his bare arms, he jumped, banging the top of his head against the ceiling.

Hairy and hot. The only two words running through the boy's mind. Everything, from the dashboard to the headrest, felt hairy like a monkey's arms, and humid blasts of gassy wind whirled around the Audi's interior.

He understood when the car growled.

"I'm in its belly," were the last words Patterson ever said out loud before eruptive hisses of stomach acid burst from out between every crack, crevice, or space big enough to fit a rodent.

The skin on Patterson's arms and legs and face dribbled off like mozzarella cheese—thin, gooey, fleshy toppings.

***

"What's going on? Where is he? You said it'd be quick," Father quipped, now holding a black attaché case in one hand.

The same case he'd hidden in the trunk of his car. The one with $20,000 in it.

Blood money.

"The beast likes to…savor the taste of its food. Give it a second," John Morty said, arms folded together, not moving.

"This better not be some bullshit or I'll have you for dinner, pal," Father snarled.

"Shut up," Morty retorted, right as the driver's-side door popped open and a loud belch came from inside.

The smell that followed was hideous. Like some zoo animal cage with manure all over the floors and bars. Father coughed and gagged, masking his nose with the bottom of his shirt. "Oh, Christ, that's awful."

"That's your son." Morty smiled and walked over to the Audi.

The car was empty and cleaned out. No Patterson, no gore, no blood, and no bones. Nothing except for a pair of car keys on the driver's seat and the irreverent bloodstain on the headrest. The beast's mark.

"Now, the payment, please," Morty replied, snatching the car keys off the seat and shutting the door.

"I almost didn't believe you. This is astounding." Father half laughed and handed over the attaché case to the car dealer.

"Nobody ever does, but now you know."

"What…what is it?"

"Agh. The question everybody wants to know. Well, I'm not exactly sure. All I do is feed the thing."

"You're joking."

"No, I'm not. But our time is up—which means you have to get going. I think you have a missing persons report to file with the local PD."

"What about my wife? We talked about her too."

"Yes, and that'll be another twenty thousand."

"It'll take a week or two, but I can get you the money."

"Take all the time in the world. I'll be here," Morty replied, flinging the white sheet back over the Audi. And then, with attaché case in hand, he strolled back to his office.

Leaving Father standing alone among the dinosaurs.

But only one real one.

A Children's Story

Ms. Kitchen's third-grade class had four long rows of wooden desks. Sunlight peeped through the window slits of the classroom like a child reaching for candy. Outside, a beautiful spring garden bloomed, and butterflies danced while the wind whistled its mighty tune.

It was a gorgeous day, and ten-year-old Phillip Driver wanted nothing more than to unhinge himself from this wretched desk, fling his writing journal across the room like a boomerang, and jump out the window.

Every bone in his prepubescent body did not want to be cooped up in here, taking this stupid, stupid test. He knew how to write and didn't need sloppy red ink marks all over his paper to tell him otherwise.

Ms. Kitchen hated the creative kids because she was no-nonsense. Phillip hated English but loved creative writing—two very different things. One was about apostrophes and commas and other useless rules, while the other was about exploring your imagination like a spaceman shooting through the galaxy in his tin metal rocket ship.

Ms. Kitchen monitored the class, walking up each aisle with the astute discipline of a sergeant inspecting the ranks. In her right hand was a long wooden ruler; on the tip of the ruler was a yellow smiley face sticker. This was Ms. Kitchen's trusty sidekick and instrument of doom. If she presumed a child was not paying attention to her lectures, she'd take the ruler and whack it across their desk.

The sound was frightening, like a bullet fired from a gun. And the look on her face was always deliciously evil. Phillip thought she liked it too much.

Ms. Kitchen had a thin frame and long neck that made her look like a bird. *Maybe a vulture or something*, thought Phillip. *Yeah, definitely. A bird that picked the flesh off the bone.* When Phillip told Don Crumb, his best friend since elementary school, that Ms. Kitchen looked like a bird, he half expected a laugh. But then Don shook his head and said that Jerry, his older brother, who'd been in Ms. Kitchen's class three long years ago, told him she was just an old dumb dried-out bitch.

Whatever that meant.

Don sat two rows across from Phillip, right near the door. His back was to Phillip, so he couldn't tell what his friend was up to, but it looked like he was busy scribbling something in his journal.

"All right, class, pencils down. That's time," Ms. Kitchen chirped. Her voice was scratchy, like an old record player. Half a second later, the ruler came flying down on top of Don's desk, jerking him up. He looked like he'd just seen a ghost or something.

"I *said*, 'Time's up.' That means you too, Don. You don't you think you're better than everyone else in the class, do you?" Ms. Kitchen said, one eyebrow perched high.

"N-no, I don't." Don fake smiled, clasping both hands together like an obedient child.

"Good." She grinned, gripping the ruler tighter. Then she turned toward the class again. "Everyone pass your papers up to the first person in each row. Do it quickly."

And everyone's papers were shuffled, collected, and then stacked on Ms. Kitchen's desk in one tall pile that looked a bit like the leaning tower of Pisa, only more smudge stains and dog-eared sheets of paper than tourists groping for their next Instagram photo post.

There was a loud knock on the door, and Ms. Kitchen walked over to answer it.

Phillip and most of the other kids couldn't help but lean over and take a peep.

When she opened the door, Phillip recognized Mr. Tremblay, their bald, oval-shaped, school principal. A lot of the kids thought he looked like Mr. Potato Head from *Toy Story*. But Phillip had his own nickname: The Egg.

Standing next to The Egg was a much shorter figure. Phillip couldn't get a good look because of the angle his desk was positioned at, but he knew it was probably another student.

There was a short exchange of conversation, some unheard words between Tremblay and Ms. Kitchen. Then Tremblay left, and Phillip heard the fat man waddle down the hallway, the soles of his shoes digging into the floor with each step.

"Well, class, this is unexpected, but we have a new student today. His name is Oscar, and he's come all the way from California. I'd like you all to give Oscar a big warm welcome," Ms. Kitchen said, one crooked hand resting on the shoulder of the student—as if she owned him now.

Oscar wore a pair of blue jean shorts and a baby blue T-shirt, looking like some artist's rendition of a perfect sunny summer afternoon. He waved back to the class sheepishly with one hand.

"Hi, Oscar," the whole class said back in tandem. Well, everyone except Phillip. His lips were glued shut, and he sank a little into his chair, sliding back so the top of the chair dug into his shoulder blades. Phillip looked around the classroom to check out everyone else's faces. Nobody moved or budged an inch…except him.

“All right, Oscar, you sit right over there next to Phillip,” Ms. Kitchen said, pointing the ruler right in Phillip’s direction. Seeing the weapon of doom directed straight at his heart instinctively snapped Phillip to attention—well, enough for him to notice the empty desk next to him.

Oscar shuffled over, moving down the aisle toward Phillip. Then he plopped himself into the desk next to him and smiled. The stench of his breath infiltrated Phillip’s nostrils like a bank robber scoping the vaults layout days before the hit.

Phillip held his nose and only breathed out his mouth, taking in large gulp fills of air all at once. Oscar reeked. He smelled like an old linen closet or mothballs that had collected under the bed. Stale and unforgiving.

But no one else seemed to notice or care.

The smell made Phillip think that maybe he was not a boy at all. Maybe Oscar was…old. For a lack of a better word. Oscar even looked like an older man with thin, bony arms and knobby elbows and pruney, dark-splotched skin. The curve of his face was sharp like a battle-ax, the brim of his nose crooked and narrow. When he smiled, Phillip saw a lifetime worth of bad hygiene: inflamed gums, likely scourged with gingivitis, and teeth rotten away.

Oscar was a ninety-year-old man. Not a ten-year-old boy by any stretch of the imagination (and Phillip prided himself on having quite an expansive one).

A part of him waited for someone else to catch on. But nobody seemed to. Phillip rubbed both eyes, as if he were clearing the dust out of them, and looked again. Nope. Still an old man.

Phillip’s arm shot up into the air.

Ms. Kitchen gave him a long, hard, cold look. “Mm. Yes, Phillip, what is it?" Her reply was distant and unforgiving. No matter what, Ms. Kitchen always hated answering anyone's questions.

"Uh." He looked at the old man. "Nothing. I forgot." Shyly, he dropped his hand down.

Ms. Kitchen rolled her eyes as if to say, "Whatever," one foot impatiently tapping the floor.

The rest of the day rolled by smoothly, though, transitioning from one scene to the next like a well-directed film.

Ms. Kitchen was Phillip's homeroom teacher, which meant that she taught all the main subjects: English, math, science, and history. Once a week, they went to PE, but that was on Fridays, and today was Wednesday.

Nobody said a word about Oscar, though. Not a peep. As if there weren't an arthritis-inflicted old man sitting in a third-grader's seat.

Sometimes, Phillip caught the old man looking around the room like he was lost somewhere. A hitchhiker stranded on the side of the highway at sunset.

A big part of Phillip wondered if this were all some big, elaborate joke. What *else* could it be? But why play a joke on Phillip? It wasn't his birthday or something fun like that. And he was not some attention-seeking kid that'd ask for something like this to happen.

Phillip just liked to write stories and envisioned being a writer someday, although he'd never told anyone that. A lot of boys his age dreamed of being football players or astronauts. That was the cliché. But not him. Wanting to be a writer was strange, like professing that you want to do homework for the rest of your life and get paid to do it.

Phillip waited out the hour and decided to wait for one more, just in case. If this all were some elaborate joke, there'd be no way it'd go on *this* long.

Then he'd for sure tell Ms. Kitchen, or one of the other kids, about Oscar. Maybe once he told somebody else, they'd see it too. Kind of like how yawns are contagious. Maybe. *Or you could wait a bit longer till lunch and ask him yourself,* Phillip thought, eyeing Oscar for the eleventh thousandth time.

He watched Oscar get up out of the desk and head over to the electric pencil sharpener. When Oscar walked, it was with a slight misstep. Kind of like he really needed a cane or walker but refused one altogether. His tiny legs were twin chicken drums with all the meat scraped off. And the backs of his calves were lined with electric blue veins and dark splotches.

Phillip watched Oscar plug a pencil into the round hole on the machine. The machine lit up and growled, grinding the pencil into a sharp spear. Oscar pulled the spear out and blew on it, giving a wide, cruel smile. One of triumph.

Then he wobbled back to the desk and went back to scribbling in his notebook.

At half past twelve, halfway through the day, Phillip had given up on the practical joke idea and wondered two things.

Number one: If all this was happening, did Oscar know that Phillip knew too? Or maybe not. Was this some game the old man liked to play? One of those secrets where someone knows that someone else knows, but both pretend like they actually don't know?

One such secret: Phillip always had a major crush on Don's older sister, Matilda, who was way far off in college somewhere. During the holidays, she'd come back and visit, and Phillip always thought she looked at him something special. You know, with that extra twinkle in her eye. All that could have been in his head, but Phillip didn't think so. Because he wanted it to be true.

Matilda was a lot older and prettier than any girl in Phillip and Don's class. And smarter too. Her first year out of high school, she went and did some mission trip in Ecuador or something and helped out. Phillip thought that was pretty cool, adult-like, and was always first to bring it up when he saw her. To get on a plane and fly far away from everything she knew—that was beyond dope. And brave. And…sexy. And a lot of other things his prepubescent body failed to navigate. Matilda was Phillip's legit first crush, and Don knew it too. But he never said anything because that was the odd game they played. Maybe Oscar was just like that.

Or number two—and this was something Phillip Driver was afraid of—he'd gone wild crazy. One time at Don's house, Don told Phillip he'd found his Dad's Netflix password, and the two of them logged on and scrolled through the movie section.

Now, this was *not* allowed, ever. Don's parents were relatively strict and monitored what their children downloaded into their brains. Nothing with foul language, violence, or inappropriate kissing stuff. That was the basic breakdown.

Even though Phillip grew up a bit differently, he wasn't allowed to watch horror movies yet unless his dad watched one with him. But everything else was basically okay. Especially with the books he read. Reading was definitely encouraged, and nothing was off limits. Last Christmas, he started getting into Stephen King's short stories and devoured them like they were prime steak and he was a hungry hyena.

When he and Don looked through Netflix, searching for something juicy, Phillip suggested a documentary on the occult. Real spooky shit.

But Don said he wasn't into stuff like that, and the two agreed on a documentary about Al Capone, the infamous gangster. That sounded like a cool idea. Guns, girls, and murder sounded something like two boys could get into.

At the end of the documentary, it said that Al Capone died crazy. Blabbering that he heard voices and saw things that weren't there. His physician told his wife that he'd caught a bug called syphilis and that it was eating his brain from the inside out.

After that, Don and Phillip shut the laptop off and didn't talk for hours. Both were kind of pale and not feeling too well. That was the last time either logged on to Don's dad's account.

The more Phillip looked over at Oscar, the more he wondered if he was sick too, just like Al Capone. Maybe the old man wasn't there *at all.* That'd definitely explain a lot. But that'd also mean Phillip would probably go crazy and die too, and that was way too scary to think about. How did one actually catch the syphilis bug? He wished the documentary had explained that one!

The class always lined up single file to go to lunch. Then, Ms. Kitchen marched them down the hall to the lunchroom. If they got too loud, they'd have to go back and start over again. Those were the rules.

Today, though, the class was quiet and obedient. Everyone was on the same wavelength and super hungry.

Phillip was a couple of kids behind Oscar in line, which was a good thing; the smell of old mothballs was a little less imposing from this distance. Once they got to the lunchroom, all the kids broke up into their various friend groups and found tables to sit at. Those that brought sack lunches from home staked their claim, marking the tables with brown bags.

Phillip and Don always sat together at a small round table in the back with some other goofy kids who were just as nerdy and geeky as they were. "Hey, uh, Don, do you notice—something—about Oscar?" Phillip said, keeping his voice to a low whisper. Careful not to wake the monster. He'd decided he'd ask Don first. Phillip trusted his friend to tell him the truth and maybe, if this wasn't some delusion, once Phillip told him, he'd see too.

Like really *see.*

"Oscar who?" Don replied, munching on a PB&J sandwich and sipping on a juice box between large, obnoxious bites.

"The new kid, Oscar!" Phillip said, biting his bottom lip.

"Oh yeah, him. Right. I forgot what his name was. Hmm. What about him?" Don replied, shrugging.

Both boys turned and look across the lunchroom. Oscar sat at a small table by himself with both elbows propped up on the table, reading a newspaper.

Or at least, that's what Phillip saw.

Don said, "He looks lonely, dude. You think we should invite him over here? It has to be hard being the new kid, especially in the middle of the semester. I wonder what his story is—probably army dad? You think?"

Phillip just stared right back at him. "You're joking right now?"

"Nah, man, joking about what? What are you taking about?"

"*Him!* Oscar. He's not—a kid!" Phillip growled, the muscles in his neck straining like flashbulbs at a fashion show in Paris.

"Whoa, man, chill out. What're you smoking? You're making noooo sense right now."

"You…really don't see it? He's over there, like, reading a newspaper. And like—he's *old.* With grey hair!"

Now Don was giving Phillip the oddest look. Like he'd just told him he'd murdered another kid and needed help getting rid of the evidence. "Right. Okay, man—yeah. I don't see anything that you're saying."

Phillip felt like he wanted to melt out of his shoes and onto the floor like a pile of goop.

"You okay, though? You look pale, dude." Don arched an eyebrow.

Phillip sighed. "Yeah…actually no. I might be going crazy. I probably have syphilis."

Don laughed, covering his mouth with one hand. "What?"

Phillip rolled his eyes. "Don't make fun of me, dude, it's not right."

"Why would *you* get syphilis?"

"I don't know, Don. Why is the sky blue? It just is."

"You don't have it, all right? Chill out. Tell me again what you see. Clarify it."

"An old man, Don. Sitting in that same seat Oscar's in. Old like your grandpa's age. I know it sounds crazy and you don't believe me, but I'm not making this up."

"All right, I believe you! But yeah, you do sound crazy, Phillip. How come I can't see him too, then?"

And Phillip thought long and hard about that. "Don't know…" Which was the absolute best answer he could give. It was the truth too.

"Well, what're you gonna do?"

"I think…I think I'm gonna talk to him at recess. I originally thought here, at lunch, but there's too many people around. I don't want anyone else thinking I'm nuts too."

"I don't think you're nuts, Phil."

"Oh, yeah, you do, Don. But whatever. I'll prove it somehow. Maybe get him to confess."

They both didn't say a word to one another for the rest of the lunch. Just silently eating.

Recess is something that cannot be planned. The mass hysteria known as a child's play time could be compared to a battlefield. Screams, yelps, and giddy hollers echoed across the playground like cries for help.

In one corner of the playground was the jungle gym, a rat trap concoction of upside-down prepubescent monkeys swinging from one bar to the next. And across from the jungle gym was a large baseball diamond with both teams skipping bases and high-fiving one another.

Phillip sat way out in the grassy field, away from the baseball diamond, practically a planet's distance from all the shouting and play. Some days, he'd seclude himself out here like some stranded sailor with a notebook and pen, riding the high seas of his imagination till a good story idea popped up.

Those were the productive days and ones he treasured immensely. They were probably also what fueled his weird, nerdy reputation, but that's another story.

Last year, Don sat with him, but now things were a bit different. His friend was definitely coming into his own, and the look on female classmates' faces said so too.

It wasn't like Phillip blamed him. After all, who *really* wanted to be that weird kid forever? Titles had a tendency to stick around some. However, Don and Phillip still sat together at lunch. Even though their dynamic had been off for a while now, Phillip didn't have the heart to bring it up to him.

Today, Don was talking to a pretty girl in their homeroom up near the baseball diamond. Although every once in a while, he'd look back at Phillip in the field, and Phillip would pretend like he didn't see his only friend giving him a pity glance.

I shouldn't have told him about Oscar. Now he thinks I'm a genuine weirdo, Phillip thought, feeling stupid for telling his friend in the first place. No one was going to believe him. Plain and simple.

Oscar sat by himself on a wooden bench on the far end of the playground, with a fat round unlit cigar clamped between his teeth and the last half of the newspaper he'd been reading at lunch inches away from his face.

But of course, nobody else except Phillip saw an old man living his glory years.

Who knew what everyone else actually saw—Don, Ms. Kitchen, The Egg Tremblay? Phillip hadn't asked his friend that, but he assumed the answer would be some vague description of another kid their age.

Phillip sighed, pushing himself off the grass. Then he began to walk across the playground toward Oscar. If there was a time better than now, Phillip didn't know when it would be.

"Hey, Oscar. Oscar!" Phillip said, stopping about five feet away from the wooden bench. His heart was beating loud in his chest, and he felt like he needed to puke all of a sudden.

The old man looked up at him and removed the cigar from between his yellow, crooked teeth. "Yeah." His voice scratchy.

"Um, yeah, hi. My name is Phillip. We sit next to each other in homeroom."

"I know you. What do you want?"

"Well...I just wanted to say that I see you. Like, *I see you*,"

Phillip spat.

But all Oscar did was fold the newspaper and flick a bony finger Phillip's way. "Oh, yeah. Well, that's what eyeballs are for, dumbass."

Phillip couldn't help but take a step back. His cheeks were flushed with red, and every limb in his body danced. "No, I mean…you're *a lot* older than everyone else. Like my grandpa."

"What're you talking about?" Now Oscar's face was twisted, every crease and wrinkle on display.

Phillip knew he'd rocked him. The jab dug into Oscar's flesh like fishhooks and was pulling him up toward the surface for everyone to see. "I don't think anyone else can see who you are. I asked a couple of people, and they looked at me like I was crazy. And for a second I thought I was, but not anymore."

"So what? Leave me alone," he grunted, putting the cigar back into his mouth.

"You admit it then!"

Oscar took the newspaper in his hand and quickly rolled it up into a tight funnel like an ice cream cone. "Tell me why I shouldn't smack you upside the head?"

"Think I'm scared of you, old man? I'm not." Phillip stood his ground, feet planted together and arms clenched into tight balls. Even though deep inside, he was petrified. Egg-shaped goosebumps ran up and down both arms. He was a parallel spaceman taking in deep breaths of moon air, spiking the flag on unclaimed alien territory.

Oscar sneered. The deep creases in his forehead were trenches now. "I'm on vacation. There, you happy now, Mr. Knower of All Things?"

At first, Phillip did not know what to say, unable to chew through his words like mice tangled in an electrical wire. But then it hit him. Boom.

It was a true revelation—a man's thoughts packed up inside an innocent boy's brain. That frightened him half to death.

And then Phillip felt the shift.

A minute ago, the world moved in slow motion. The orange sun burned bright energy beams down from the heavens, and birds chirped to one another, singing each other's praises.

But now—

Phillip squinted through the haze. He saw the world through a milky eyeglass that stretched for miles and miles. Everything—the playground, the blacktop, his friends—seemed far away. Panic greeted him like a familiar friend. "A vacation from—being old? That's not possible."

"When you're older, you'll understand. My family left me to rot in a retirement home. Because everyone thinks: What good are the elderly? They don't work or contribute anymore. I guess I finally got fed up with it, kid, to tell you the truth."

Oscar grinned, twisting the grin into a crooked spear. A hate storm hiding behind long, cruel wrinkles and thinning silver hair. It was the most horrible look Phillip had seen in his life. Scarier than any R-rated monster movie he watched behind his mother's back.

This was a real pain. And it all descended onto Phillip, knocking him over. Phillip wanted nothing more than to feel the warmth of his mother's embrace. Childlike again. Innocent.

"The older you get, the less people care. The more you want to go back…but you can't. We're all destined to become ghosts in a graveyard." Oscar's joints click-clacked when he moved, sounding like rotten, squeaky floorboards.

Phillip had thought his body would never make those noises in a million years. But now he understood that one day his body would. Everybody got older and died alone.

And there was nothing he could do, either. One day, it'd be his turn. The existential fear grabbed hold and shook him silly, shooting lightning bolts into his spine. Reality was caving in—time choking itself with murderous strength.

All Phillip wanted to do was forget. But it was too late for that.

"Now, go on, boy!" Oscar took the cigar in his hand and pressed the red ember end against Phillip's cheek, holding it until the boy cried out in pain. The pain was unbearable—a white-hot sun shooting hundreds of arrows into his solar plexus.

Last year, his family had moved into a new home. The location of the home and how much money they'd needed to invest to fix her up was looked over a million times. Phillip's family had always been brilliant with finances—but this was different.

For starters, the kitchen and dining room floor needed retiling, and the bathroom plumbing needed to be reconfigured so brown splurges of shit didn't eject out of the pipes like Armageddon every time somebody pushed the handle down. Then there were the possums and raccoons running rampant in the backyard and a hornet army buzzing under the floorboards.

To save money, Phillip's father decided to do most of the renovations himself. Uprooting tile, tightening rusty pipes, and chasing out animals with various chemical sprays, gizmos, and gadgets. Phillip liked being around his father when he worked. Hammering, sweating, the occasional curse, being real manly. One day, Phillip decided to help out and pick up a hammer and nail—accidentally driving the tip of the nail right through the doughy flesh of his palm. Just like Jesus.

Impaling himself hurt a lot but was nothing compared to having a stogie put out on his face. When the red-hot tip kissed Phillip's cheek, fireworks exploded in his head. He saw all colors, big bright paparazzi flashbulb reds, blues, and yellows.

"OWWW!"

When Phillip hit the ground, it sounded like a sack of cement. But he was quick to his feet. Galloping across the blacktop, snot oozing down his nose and hot cheeks.

Trying not to think of the horror behind him. Or hear the old man's cackling laughter.

A Fairy-Tale Ending

Meg loved Leonard.

Leonard Grover was the boy with good hair but bad intentions. Writer. Artist. Poet. And wordsmith. He carried a silver switchblade in one pocket and a leather-bound notebook in the other. Meg's sixteen-year-old mind dreamed of fantastical things with that boy. Marriage, babies, grandchildren.

If only.

Meg's loneliness and desperation to find her prince had brought her more agony than any amount of actual physical pain ever could. She knew now that the human heart was just a muscular organ about the size of a fist and that it was the heart's job to pump blood through a network of arteries and veins in the cardiovascular system.

Nothing more, nothing less. It wasn't some magical portal to never-ending happiness. And it sure as hell didn't hold the secrets to life, love, and purpose. That was nonsensical fluff that belonged in the movies and fairy tales.

Some nights, Meg dreamed of taking a carving knife and cutting her heart out— just to see what the organ of a heartbroken woman looked like. She imagined it black and charcoaled, like a cancerous lung.

When she swiveled around, everything about her bedroom felt alien. The edge of the nightstand stuck out like a serrated silver knife in the utensil drawer, eager to pierce flesh. And the ceiling fan in her room hung too low, nearly at neck-chopping level.

Her mother's personal items, and many memories of Meg's childhood, had been regurgitated all over the floor. Picture frames, hardback books, and school clothes.

Meg picked up one of the fat books. On the front cover in big, blood-red letters: *The Complete Fairy Tales* by Hans Christian Andersen. She didn't have to open the book to read the stories; by the time Meg turned thirteen, she could recount Andersen's works by memory.

Her mother always told Meg that every girl deserved a fairy-tale ending and that one day, she would meet someone that personified a storybook hero. You know, that knight in shining armor that climbed the tower to rescue the princess. He would be clad in silver and would slay dragons with the sword worn in a scabbard on his hip. This man would do anything to meet Meg, to kiss her lips. And once he arrived, it was Meg's job not to let him go.

"Tell me a fairy tale, Leonard. But put you and me in it." Meg blushed, her warm lips on the phone receiver and one finger wrapped around the curly cord. She liked their talks. Leonard spoke like there was an ink pen in his hand at all times. His words were beautiful and seductive.

"I wrote a story about you and me. It's about how we would've met in another life." Leonard's voice sent seismic waves through her groin.

"Oh…a fairy tale? Well, I hope you're the daring knight come to rescue me."

"That's exactly what I wrote. Wow, it's like you read my mind." Leonard chuckled. His hearty laugh nearly toppled the young teen over.

"Tell me! Read it over the phone," Meg said, bits of spittle flying from her lips, beyond excitement that could not be contained.

So Leonard did, putting down the phone to snatch up his notebook.

“Well, I was walking in a haze. The kind of fog you might stumble through on the hardest narcotic, even though I was sober as a bird doing flips in the air. But deep inside me, I knew why I felt this way. It’s one of those things you just feel but don’t have the words to describe it because the human language hasn’t invented a word for it yet. When I looked around, I was standing in a field. This field was filled with green grass that licked my knees and tickled like the bristles of a toothbrush. At the end of the field stood a tall brick spiral tower. Maybe five or six stories high. The base of this tower was wrapped with thick vines and covered with small black critters like bugs, beetles, and caterpillars. When I approached the spiral cone, I looked up and saw a mop of pretty blonde hair hanging off the top of the tower like a flag in the wind. The blonde mop belonged to a beautiful woman with clear skin and baby blue eyes. It was clear this woman wanted the attention of me, the dumb, dazed, reluctant white knight.

“She said, ‘I’m lonely and don’t want to live any longer. Every minute of this existence is hell! Climb this tower and rescue me from misery, or I’ll jump.’

“And I knew the woman was serious. She had a look that spoke volumes. Her eyes followed the bright blue horizon until it ran out of color, like they were searching for heaven.

“I told her, ‘Don’t jump! I’m coming up.’ My imagination was drawing gruesome pictures with blood-red crayons. But then, I stepped and heard a crunch beneath my boot. The crunch was loud, like a hundred eggs being cracked in some mad scientist’s experiment. When I looked down, there was yolk on my heel. It was thick and sticky and came up in long, thin, gooey strands. And it smelled like curdled milk. The goop came from the white bone goblet that was somebody’s skull. Pieces of the shattered skull were all around me. Strewn about in the tall green grass.

"There were other bits of human remains too. Little bone fragments that looked like the tops of fingers and toes. Then I saw a portion of spine and spiky vertebrae. Whatever meat had clung to those bones had rotted or been torn off. It was clear to me this skeleton belonged to another man. They all did.

"You see, there were other dead men too. And their twisted and broken bodies were everywhere. The more I kicked through the tall grass, the more I found. Like a childhood Easter egg hunt with a dark twist. All these men had died climbing the tower. The tall foreboding brick beast of a mountain, built with hardened palms and bloody hands. And I knew why. It was all for—her. This woman was born a prisoner. And on a planet populated by parading knights on horseback, she was the ultimate prize.

"I don't know why I started the climb. Risking my life for…her? This was just a woman, a bloody woman. If I turned around and walked away, eventually I'd forget all about the woman and the godforsaken tower. This memory would eventually become a misty fog that swims around my brain like goldfish in a dirty bowl. But before I knew it, I was already halfway up the tower. Hand over hand, pressed against the cold brick wall like a boxed sardine. The soft curls of wind up there licked my cheek and dried my eyes. I watched a bead of sweat drop off my chin and fall to the abyss below. It waved goodbye with a tearful salute…"

Meg wanted to climb through the phone and jab Leonard with her tongue, to have him for forever and always. Her heavy breathing asphyxiated the receiver.

"After an hour of climbing, I finally topped the tower, and the woman came toward me with a hungry heart. Hard of breath, I asked for her name, and she told me…"

"Meg," Meg and Leonard uttered simultaneously.

"And we kissed until our lips fell off. My tongue explored her mouth and vice versa. Real-life ecstasy pills with a beating heart and bloodstream. None of us could help the desire behind our eyes."

"Megan? Megan, are you all right?" another voice bellowed. This one louder than the one in her own head. Which made Meg open her eyes again, ejecting her from the memory of her conversation with Leonard. Of the love she'd lost.

And back to her room. And the other boy (not Leonard) who sat beside her like a choirboy, his hands clasped together in a nonthreatening manner.

Mac.

Mac was the type of boy you forgot about. The one that sat in the back of the classroom and didn't say much. Not too handsome but not too ugly either. The Macs of the world tended to float in and out of the human psyche like ghosts.

Meg's parents loved Mac and hated Leonard. Mac was safe. He didn't drink or get into trouble. He didn't party and cause trouble with the law. Boys like him made good grades and ended up going to good schools.

Even though they were boring.

Mac adjusted himself on the bed, taking in Meg's gorgeous five-foot-nine frame. She was tall, with slim tan legs and round eyes. "Meg," the boy murmured, taking the time to formulate his words, etching them like an artist. "I think that you and I have something special."

But Meg cut him off with a hard stare. "I want...Leonard. You're not what I asked for at all."

Mac didn't blink. The electrical circuit in the android's head computed her tone and matched it with an image of a barking dog. "You're annoyed?" he replied softly.

Mac didn't have a brain, but it wasn't rocket science as to why the girl didn't like him. They were different, one flesh and blood, the other nuts and bolts. However, he'd been designed for her, and the neglect hurt a little.

"You're angry at me, Megan?" Mac Bot replied, his heat sensors picking up blasts of steam that shot out her nose like a bull. Frustrated air vents.

"You're an android, Mac. Bought and assembled by my parents to keep me happy. But you're not real—and I'm in love with someone else," Meg cackled while chewing on her lip to stop the tears from flowing.

But Mac didn't understand.

A couple of Megan's friends from school were going out with androids. It was the newest, hottest craze. All the teens were doing it. Androids didn't cheat or break your heart or leave you waiting in the rain on a movie date. And they never broke up with you—the things stuck around like flies on shit. Everyone wanted an android…except Meg.

"Go tell my parents I don't want you anymore. They won't listen to me," the girl griped, facing away from Mac.

"You know I can't do that, Megan. Why don't we watch a movie together? I'm sure we can find something you like."

"No! I'm so sick of you." Meg bounced off the bed and went for the door, twisting the locked doorknob hard to no avail.

Stuck.

“It’s past curfew, Megan. You know you’re not allowed outside.”

“Shut up!”

Mac Bot didn’t say a word. Instead, he booted up the laptop and began scrolling through Netflix, thumbing different genres and types of movies. “Have you seen *The Blackcoat’s Daughter*? You like horror, don’t you, Megan?”

Meg flipped around and went for a wall outlet where a lengthy snakelike auxiliary cable dangled out. The same cable connected to Mac Bot’s back. “My parents think they can make me a Prince Charming from scratch—well, fuck them!” She yanked Mac’s life support out of the wall and watched Mac collapse onto the floor in one dusty heap. A scatterbrained junk box of wires and gizmos.

Then the outlet exploded and the lights in Megs bedroom flickered on and off.

“Consider this a breakup, Mac.” Meg laughed, jumping back a little to avoid irreverent hot sparks. The corners of her lips pulled back into a meaty smile.

Ten seconds later, all hell broke loose.

A fire-breathing dragon roared from down below, using its hind legs to storm up the hallway staircase that led to the girl’s room. “Godammit, Meg!” her father belched. Coming quick and fast.

But Meg was quicker, vaulting over to her bookshelf and using every bit of her strength to push it in front of the door. “Try locking me in, huh! Well I’ll lock you OUT!” she screamed, hearing her father’s breathing outside the door, his fists banging on the frame.

“Meg! Did you unplug another android!”

"Mac's faulty, Dad, we gotta send him back!" She eyed the unresponsive android splayed out on the floor.

"No, he's not! Your mother and I paid good money for Mac. He's the best boyfriend unit out right now. So you're going to like him!"

"Well, he's dead, Dad! Gone to android heaven." Meg sneered, picturing her father red faced with snot dribbling down his pointed chin. The image made her happy—like Leonard Grover.

Next, she went to her bedroom window and popped the screws out. It took a while, but despite her father's loud thumping on the door, he wasn't getting in any time soon.

After Meg lifted the window up and the cool night air danced on her earlobes, her father's fist bumping stopped. "Meg, I can hear the window. If you're thinking about going to see that boy, forget about it. He's trouble."

"His name's Leonard, Dad, and you can't tell me what to do anymore!"

Hopping out her bedroom window and down the rain gutter was easy; she'd done it a million times before. First, Meg wrapped her arms around the tin spout and then used both legs to act as braces in case she fell. In thirty seconds, she was on the ground, dusting rose bush petals off her knees, trying not to laugh while imagining her father pounding on the door like a madman.

The moon shone down on the neighborhood block like a flashlight—soft silvers and grays illuminating Meg's world.

So she ran.

Arms pumping. Legs going. Fueled by a belligerent fire in her belly that only the youth know, because the adults have forgotten.

Sweet, beautiful, but misunderstood Leonard. The prince in her fairy tale. The one who rode in on a Harley instead of a horse. Meg loved him, and nobody or nothing could replace him.

The tingle between her thighs said so. Meg felt wanted for the first time in her life. And that feeling was incredible, like losing one's virginity in an endless loop. In her mind, Leonard was a knight with dirt on his boots and riding chaps underneath his clothes. And his silver chain mail armor and sword were probably hidden somewhere behind a tree, ready for battle at a moment's notice.

She ran harder, faster.

It took twenty minutes to get to Leonard's house. And by the time she did, she was doused in sweat and dirt and breathing like a capsized sea fisherman. Eyes shut. Hunched over. But thrilled nevertheless.

Leonard's house light was on and burning brightly in the night; in her mind, it was a lighthouse beacon in a shifting storm.

Meg gathered her senses and rang the doorbell. Trying to remind herself to keep breathing. In. Out. In. Out…

The front door suddenly swung open, and the man in the doorway greeted her with his eyes. They were round and sweet like two donuts.

"Sorry, who are you?" In contrast to his beady eyes, the stranger's voice was tough, like unfiltered cigarettes and rusty nails spiked into wooden bats. He was twenty years older than Meg but wore it well in the face.

But his horrid looks weren't the most unique thing about him. The man was truly an anomaly. That one asteroid that snuck through Earth's red-hot barrier and would now obliterate the human race. Nothing about the man made sense. Not from the head down anyhow.

The man's thin and frail frame paled in comparison to his handsome face, which was packed with the fullness and vigor of somebody much younger.

Meg was quick to notice the bony knobs of his elbows and knees sticking through the fabric of his suit jacket and pants. To her, it truly looked like he hadn't eaten in weeks. His emaciated arms and legs reminded her of a chicken wing with all the meat slurped off the bone. Meg imagined a grave robber. One that dug up freshly buried corpses and then took a hacksaw and bagged the pieces he liked. But that thought was morbid and ridiculous, so she quickly dismissed it.

"Um, hi…Mr. Grover. Is Leonard home?" Meg mumbled, nervously chewing on her lip. One foot over the other. Forgetting how strong she'd been just a minute ago. She had now morphed back to her shy teen self—a girl in love, a girl with numerous insecurities.

"What do you want with Leonard?" Mr. Bag Of Bones spat, one eyebrow curiously cocked.

"I'm Leonard's girlfriend. Well, I used to be. My parents broke us up."

"That's impossible."

Meg didn't know what to say or do. Caught up in a whirlpool. "Yes it is. What do you mean?

"*I'm* Leonard!"

Meg didn't have time to finish her panicked thought. Because someone, an unknown entity, came up behind her and flipped the toggle switch on the back of her neck, which in turn dropped the android girl to her knees. And, just like the Mac Bot, also shut her off.

The unknown entity, an older man in a lab coat with a handlebar mustache and slicked-back grey hair, sighed deeply and then sucked oxygen in like a vacuum. "Aye, sorry about that, Leonard. The bot got out. My wife and I are still working a few kinks out in the system."

"Yeah, well, the damned thing scared me half to death. Christ, her looking all googly-eyed—"

"You don't have to worry about one thing, Mr. Grover. The Meg Bot is one of our newer models, completely wireless, and once she's fully functional…well, you'll be a pleased customer."

"How'd she find me?" Leonard grunted.

"Well, since were are in the middle of programming right now, we're feeding the bot all your information and downloading every fairy tale about a handsome prince into her memory bank. I think—well, because of the information overload, she's grown quite smitten with you, Mr. Grover. Concocted a fantasy for herself. She thinks you're James Dean or some storybook charmer."

This news made the skeletal man perk up, a sleazy, greasy grin covering his lips now. One formed by years of loneliness, shame, and a desire for the forbidden flesh. "Good. For what I paid, her pussy better be tighter than an elevator. Your company promised me the best sex bot on the market." Leonard cackled.

This made Meg's father laugh too. "Oh, you will be pleased, Mr. Grover. My wife and I are training her with our Mac Bot to ensure she's well equipped to handle…anything you desire."

He bent over to scoop up Meg's lifeless circuit sack and put her in the back seat of his car parked in the driveway.

It was back to the lab.

There was still work to be done.

When It's Dark Out

Everyone has their secrets.

Crispin Charles took his wedding ring off. Then he turned the car off and let the engine rattle itself to sleep. The motel, a seedy hunk of junk located right off the interstate, housed more grimy creatures than human beings—swamp things with red eyes and talons ready to rip their prey to shreds.

Only the underbelly of society swapped cash for room keys here. Drug dealers, prostitutes, convicted felons, junkies looking for their next fix…and unfaithful spouses. Thirty-five-year-old Crispin used his throwaway phone to throw out a cosmic fishhook through digital space. "*I'm here*," he texted. Waited.

Five seconds later, he reeled in the big catch.

"*Room 211.*"

Boom.

And there it was, the virtual handshake. A hello from one deprived cannibal to another, both ready to devour the other whole, slurping meat from the bone. Every bud on Crispin's tongue ached to suck the satisfaction sap off her lips. He craved his mystery woman like tomorrow's sunrise.

Catherine Keeper wanted to cry, to blow nitroglycerin tears down both cheeks. She could not evade the awful feeling of dread that crawled up her spine like a spider. Then she saw a blare of bright headlights whip into the motel parking lot and knew the car belonged to…him.

“His name is Crispin,” she said to herself. Reciting the younger man’s name like she knew him…but that was the lie they shared, pretending all this was one hot, steamy scene from a play. All that jazz is fun online, but reality hits hard, like a heavyweight boxer.

For one year now, Catherine had toyed with the idea of killing herself. Like really doing it. Either with a rope or a gun. And Crispin did not know *that.*

He did not know a lot of things.

Such as how Catherine whacked all the mirrors in her apartment with a ball peen hammer until it felt like her whole world had been flipped and shaken like a childhood bully emptying some poor kid’s pockets for lunch money.

Like how Catherine knew she was pretty but not gorgeous anymore. And the other anorexic pale-faced twenty-somethings she saw in the street confirmed it. The looks on their faces were water in the desert to young men—pure lust. At one point, Catherine had possessed the power too, with her pouty lips, eight ball–round dark eyes, and shoulder-length wavy brown hair. In her youth, all she needed was a witch’s hat and broomstick to complete the Halloween outfit. Not that she denied the similarities back then, with her ruby-red amulet bracelets, silver earrings, and jingling medieval necklaces hanging off her throat. It was just the right amount of rock and roll.

But not anymore; at forty-four, Catherine was outdated. A Windows 95 computer in an iPhone 10 world. Forgotten.

When Catherine opened the motel door to let him in, he stood there. Crispin was taller than she expected, well over six feet, with broad shoulders and a granite chin. And when he spoke to her, his voice was gentlemanly, but also rough too—just the way she liked it.

Then she saw the black gym bag slung over his shoulder, and her pelvis tingled. There was probably a rope or handcuffs in there—along with other off-market toys. Real freaky shit. For weeks, they'd talked about him tying her up—and much more. Crispin said it was mandatory.

A part of the process.

"Well, Catherine, you're even more gorgeous in person," he said, unable to hide the nervousness in his throat. Truth be told, he probably came off more like a schoolboy in the principal's office than a seductive slick talker ready to handle business. But that was okay—she looked uneasy too. They were both a couple of rubber ducks bobbing aimlessly in the bathwater.

"Oh, thank you, Crispin." She blushed, her cheeks a warm, rosy red. No handsome guy had ogled her like that since she'd turned forty. The way he stared her down like a piece of meat sent flying sparks to her nether region once again. This man checked all the boxes and more.

She was ready.

"Can I get you a drink?" she asked. "There's a mini bar with soda, gin, and ice."

"I don't drink." Crispin walked past her and slung the duffel bag onto the probably cockroach-infested bed. Then he sat on the end of it, and the steel springs under the mattress sneezed. For the first time, he got a good look at the room: small and low rent, with a dusty bed, a television set, and a derelict bathroom. But this would make do for the night. It had to.

A moment of undeniable silence wafted through the room before Crispin spoke up again.

"But...I'd like you to know what I'm thinking about." The way he welded his words together was a sniper scope aimed right at her chest.

“Tell me, please. I’m begging you,” she murmured, tasting it on her tongue. And oh boy, was it the sweetest pleasure.

“Well, a part of me wants to believe this real and not just some perverted dream. And that any moment now I won’t wake up back in bed with my fat wife and our stupid kids sleeping down the hall. I pray that doesn’t happen.”

At that moment, Catherine had never wanted another man so desperately in her whole life. Because she would be his thrilling escape from the mundane, and the idea of that was overwhelming. Yes, they’d talked about Crispin’s “other life” a hundred thousand other times, but hearing all this in person was…different? And to see the rage smoke pouring out of his eyes, ears, and tightly clenched fists. His hate was a passion that burned brighter than a shooting star. God, it was beautiful.

“I’m not going anywhere, Crispin. Nobody else on the planet understands you like I do.” And she meant it. So when he unzipped the duffel bag and pulled out an ice pick, a kitchen knife, a long thin piece of piano wire, a rope, and fat roll of duct tape, she was not bothered one bit.

They’d talked a million times over about how he planned to kill her.

Catherine took the ice pick and touched its shiny silver point. The thing was sharp and would pierce through flesh easily. One quick stab to the jugular or other major artery, and she would bleed out like a stuck pig, no squealing. She put the ice pick down and gripped the twelve-inch knife by the handle, slashing it in the air with an imaginary fatal swoop.

“Whoa, easy there, Michael Myers. You act like you’ve never seen a knife before.” Crispin laughed. He sat comfortably on the bed; on his face was the smile of someone dipping their foot into warm bathwater. All the built-up tension and nervousness from before—suddenly gone.

“Yeah, I have. But not one that’s going to be used on…me.”

“Are you afraid?”

“I’m more afraid of the pain than actually dying. Does that makes sense?”

“Oh, one hundred percent. I actually brought you something that’ll take care of the problem.” Crispin whipped out a medicine bottle with a white cap. Then he shook it, and twenty 2.5 mg Percocet tablets hissed like baby rattlesnakes. “Ever taken one before?”

“No.” Catherine let the lie slip through her teeth, pretending pills had never mixed well with wine and late-night TV. To admit that would be…unattractive. Sloppy.

“Can I tell you a silly secret?” Crispin’s lips moved in tandem—perfect pink plumps. He set the pill bottle on the bed next to sister ice pick and brother knife.

“Yes…anything you want to tell me.”

“Sometimes I chew on my lip to taste the blood. Only, the thing is…I like to pretend it’s someone else’s.”

“Do you want to cut me?” The words spilled out from Catherine’s lips and hovered around the duo like mosquitos. Not even the world’s strongest bug repellent could keep them away.

“Oh God…yes,” Crispin gobbled, his Adam’s apple bobbing up and down, riding the eternal wave. Then he gripped the kitchen knife tightly and stood up. The primordial beast inside him awakened: red bells ringing, sound the alarm.

“Tease me, please.” Catherine held her arm out, rolled up the sleeve slowly.

A tease. Which meant, like a movie trailer, there was more to come. The hot iron burden of masquerading his sickness was…over? God, that felt incredible.

He cut her really good, driving the dagger horizontally across her forearm, leaving a long, thin, bloody trail of flesh tears. Fuck, the damn thing hurt, but Catherine was determined to take the pain like a champ.

The way he looked at her was ecstasy. Like a million other naked younger women could be standing outside, waiting to please him—*but it wouldn't matter*. He possessed *her*, as one would possess a potted plant, a painting, or a Porsche.

He almost came while cutting her. No lie. And then watching her blood drip onto the carpet to stain it like a wine commercial was something else. When he eventually extinguished the life from her eyes, it would be the single greatest moment of his life.

No rush, though. They'd both get there.

"Oh, damn. Let's patch you up now." Crispin reached for the duct tape in his duffel bag and ripped off a generous piece with his teeth. Then he took her arm and wrapped it like a leaky pipe, shutting the thing off for good.

"What a gentleman," Catherine said, blushing apple red. If someone had turned the thermostat all the way up, she would've been the last one to notice.

"Did that hurt more or less than you thought it would?" He couldn't keep his eyes off her now.

"Mm, I won't lie. It hurt…but I liked it a lot, so that made up for the pain."

"Should…we try the ice pick next time? I had this batshit crazy idea of stabbing you in the neck with it like Sharon Stone did in

Basic Instinct. But—that might kill you quick though, so maybe not. Ha-ha." Crispin talked liked a schoolboy.

Catherine felt that too and thought it was sexy. To her, one of the more appealing things about serial killers was their motivations. "Maybe later. I want to know about you, Crispin," she said, suddenly wishing they were at a nice restaurant with an ocean view or something romantic instead of a stinky old motel room. Maybe meeting this brilliant, dark stranger over the internet was the greatest thing that had ever happened to her…

"Ask away." His words were honey.

"Who are your favorite serial killers of all time? I'm dying to know."

"Hmm. Like *the* best, or my personal preference? Those are two different questions."

"Both," she said with a slight crackle in her voice.

"Karl Denke is the Michael Jordan of killers, for sure. He wrote the hunt-and-stalk bible. But Ted Bundy and Gary Ridgway are my favorites."

"Denke? Have I heard of him?"

"Denke was a Prussian serial killer and cannibal who killed *hundreds* of homeless people in the early twentieth century." Crispin's face lit up like a pumpkin on Halloween.

"How?"

"With knives, hammers, axes, stuff like that."

"And Bundy? Ridgway?"

"Oh, them. Well, Bundy might be the modern textbook case for serial killers. If Denke's MJ, he's LeBron or Wilt Chamberlain.

Totally came in and fucked the game up. Then Ridgway, who everyone knows as the Green River Killer, well, he tied his victims up and strangled them."

Catherine was totally enthralled by this morbid stranger; her eyes lit up like fireflies. "Can I ask you another question, Crispin?"

"Yeah, shoot."

"Why do you want to kill…*me*?"

"Well, I like you, and I'd like to remember you. Everyone remembers their first."

"Oh." She squinted. "So, you want to kill again? You didn't mention that online is all…"

"Yeah, well, I don't know. It depends on the variable." Crispin looked away, frustrated now, his thoughts on a hamster wheel.

But Catherine knew what he was talking about. The variable, or rather, the ball and chain sharing his last name, Mrs. Charles. His wife. Catherine immediately regretted bringing the bitch up. Mentioning his "other" life was like throwing a bucket of ice water on someone drifting through a beautiful dream. The whole point of tonight was about enacting fantasies, not reliving daily trauma.

"Bundy's got nothing on you," she quipped, scooping up the ice pick with a playful "I'm sorry" pout on her lips. And it worked.

Crispin grabbed the pick and laughed, then flipped it so that he was holding it by the spike tip, and butted her in the chest with the wood handle. "OK. Take your clothes off. And do it slowly." His satisfaction came from watching her peel each layer of clothing off like an onion. But his pleasure was not the sexual kind—more like getting a good whiff of a delicious dinner in the oven. Crispin longed to spill her blood and wipe it on the walls and windows.

Catherine, on the other hand, wanted him to take her then and there. Then her pupils were enlarged black marble stones, filled to the brim with pure ecstasy. When she unhooked her silk black bra and panties, she did the deed slowly, letting her lingerie fall to the floor with a mating call rattle and shake of her hips. Then she lay down on the bed.

"Good. Now for the rope." Crispin had learned about sailor knots from binging YouTube videos. First he did her wrists, looping the rope around them. Then her legs. "Okay. Test my work!" he said, super excited. Game time. Nothing could stop the insatiable appetite for destruction his soul housed. All this was fun for Crispin—a demented Disneyland. Tigers hunted antelope on the wild plain, so why couldn't he?

"Nope. I'm stuck, honey. You did good." Her lie caught on the tip of her tongue, doing a tasteful tango. The truth was, he hadn't tied the ropes *that* well. She could wiggle her wrists and probably get away *if* she wanted to…but that wasn't a part of the fantasy they'd created together.

So a little lie was in order.

"No, the YouTube tutorials did. Now, pick your favorite flavor of ice cream," he said, scooping up the ice pick in one hand and the knife with his other.

"Hmm…you choose, but just remember to cut deep so I die quickly."

"I was thinking right through the heart. Or is that too dramatic?"

"Not if you love me, Crispin." Her words rebounded off the motel walls like a child in an inflatable bouncy castle. Only this was not a kid's game, and the night's stakes were balanced on a tightrope between life and death.

"What?"

"I said—"

But Crispin cut her off. "No, yeah, I heard what you said. Why would someone stab somebody they loved to death? That doesn't make any sense."

And there it was. Enough to make Catherine shut her eyes, exhale, and fight through the deafening silence. "God damn you, Crispin."

"Huh?"

"Why do you think I'm doing this?"

"Doing what? *This.* Like letting me tie you up and—"

"Yes! The motel rendezvous, that knife, the pick, this rope, our plan. ALL OF IT. Because it was your idea! You talked about Ted Bundy online like he cured cancer, and I listened. Tonight, this moment is for *you*. Use me."

Crispin said nothing, knew nothing. And Catherine saw through the scenario without a CAT scan. It was the dead quiet atmosphere in the room that did not want to rest in peace.

"Who did you think I was?" she asked. "A deranged mental patient off her meds, or some suicidal sap for you to play with?

"Neither," Crispin lied, wishing he could kill her now without sacrificing his high. All the girls he butchered *wanted* it! And knowing that glued the fantasy together.

"Liar!"

Think, he told himself. *Give her...something.* But Crispin couldn't. Whatever useless lie rested on his lips like a virus turned rotten. God damn the old bitch to hell. In fact—no, hell would be too good for someone like *her*. Crispin wanted to pry her smart mouth open with pliers and remove that nasty tongue. Hot, steaming, red rage mixed with adrenaline. Did shit like this ever happen to Bundy? Or Gacy? The Ripper? Nope!

Then the world flipped.

“That’s what I thought. So untie me, asshole,” Catherine said.

Her silver-toothed tongue was a wicked serpent riding a stormy sea wave back home. Hurt. Outside, the night wind whistled and moaned, rocking tree branches to sleep. Crispin felt dirty, like a lizard lying beneath a rock. More monster than man, half his mind burning rubber down an endless maniacal highway.

“Huh? What? No—that’s not—you—y-you—*can’t do that*!” he stuttered. Knuckles snow white. Wanting to beat her now. Beat her and then kill her and stick a stake in her and revive her like Frankenstein, just to do it all over again.

“I do whatever I want! Let go!” Catherine screamed, her naked breasts popping up and down. On top of her, he could feel her heartbeat dropping music beats. Loud, thunderous booms.

So Crispin hit her. But Catherine hit back harder. First she broke her wrist bind, and then she gripped the ice pick like Thor’s hammer and swung up.

Staking it right through his neck.

Crispin didn’t feel the stick right away, no sir, but the knuckle sandwich intended for her went away, shrinking to silly putty. And the look he wore was a Pulitzer Prize–winning photo, a superfluous harmony between life and death.

Like a white shirt with blue jeans, death never goes out of style. But medically speaking, death happens in two stages. The first stage is clinical death, which lasts for three to five excruciating minutes when a person stops breathing and their heart stops pumping blood. When this is happening, a person's organs are still going, and oxygen is pumped through the brain.

But it's the second stage of dying that strikes fear into the hearts of all. In biological death, the organs stop, and heaven and hell are a breath away. After this, rigor mortis sets in, making the body taut and hard. And unless that person's body is embalmed, it will start decomposing as soon as blood stops flowing. When the tissue rots, maggots, bugs, and even roaches consume most of the carcass.

Whatever else remains is reflected in the glint of the reaper's blade.

Flash Fiction Stories

A Perfect World

He gripped the power drill with one hand and the doorknob with the other, and inserted the tip of the drill through the lock. Unsurprisingly, the thing went through like a knife cutting through warm butter. In one side and out the other.

When the bedroom door swung open, his heart hopped; in front of him was a beautiful dark nothing void that seemed to stretch for miles and miles.

He barely heard the sleeping couple's snores or the bounce of his feet on the floorboards tip-tapping into Hell.

The black leather jacket, pants, boots, and ski mask he wore weren't his idea. Nothing about the "uniform" turned him on or made him happy. In fact, the word *uniform* was unsettling. In his mind, people who worked shitty jobs in warehouses or fast food joints wore uniforms. And although going to work in one's uniform paid the bills, it wasn't fun, or empowering, or freeing. It was just a means to an end.

But sadly, killing was more similar to a nine-to-five job than one would expect. If he didn't wear his uniform to work, the consequences could be dire. Any left-behind hair fiber or skin cells were potential evidence for the CSI boys. And that he couldn't have.

In a perfect world, he did it nude. Bare to the bone, like a baby. Nothing separating him from the bloody carnage.

Wanting to do the job nude wasn't so much of a sexual thrill as it was breaking the process down to the way it *ought* be done. Man to man. One on one. Flesh touching flesh. Kill or be killed.

The couple in the bedroom was older. Maybe sixty. Both wore flannel pajamas, looking like something out of a AARP catalogue.

The murder had been mapped out meticulously in his head. First, he'd smother the wife with her own goose feather pillow and then use the power drill on the husband. He'd dig deep down into the part of the brain that dictated motor function and render him a vegetable for life. It was some real sick and twisted horror novel shit. The kind of stuff he liked to read for leisure.

But—

That was the fantasy. This was as far as he'd ever gone before. Ever. Right now, in this dark room with the sleeping couple who were blissfully unaware of certain bloody scenes blooming in his beautiful head.

And it was as far as he would probably ever go. On the cliff's edge overlooking the abyss. Leaning forward but not actually falling in.

"In a perfect world, though, I could," he whispered while tracing his finger around the bed's edge. "I could go all the way…but the journey is more thrilling than the destination. If I killed you both, well, I'd probably want to do it again. And again. But it would never be as good as the first time. So it's better this way."

He snickered and clipped the power drill back on his belt. He stayed for another minute. Imagining everything he'd do. Eyes closed. Legs locked. In the zone.

Just knowing he could was enough.

Then he left through the front door, his hot breath coming out like a cloud of city smog against the outside air.

Everything as it should be.

Pigeon

Most people think death is a long way away. They participate in high-risk behavior like it doesn't matter. Like the gods turn a blind eye to our stupidity.

Others become obsessed with it, wondering when and how the deed will be written. And will it be painful? Or scary? Or painfully dull and drawn out like art classes with no paper?

Melanie adjusted her sundress and wiggled her toes to shake the sandals on her feet. *It's too beautiful of a day to die, and that's what makes it perfect*, the fifteen-year-old thought, peering over the building ledge with interest. Blue skies. No rain. No clouds. No planes. No people telling her to stop.

But it wouldn't be picture-perfect summer for long. Because every bird has to fly south for the winter, and this pigeon was headed straight down…

Twenty-one-year-old Jonathan was handsome. Blond-haired, blue-eyed, with a grin like a great white shark, thin hips, broad shoulders, and a tall imagination to boot. Melanie couldn't get enough of him, mainlining the boy with a junkie's enthusiasm.

She loved him, and today they were dying together.

"Are you ready, Melanie? It's just you and me now," Jonathan whispered. He stood beside her, in a pair of leather boots and an oversized hoodie with tattered holes on the sleeves and neck. Grunge without the desperation. But even Captain Cool couldn't resist the urge to peer over into the abyss. To get a good look at the devil before he shook hands with him.

“Ye…s. I’m ready, Jonathan. As long as you’re going with me.” Melanie licked her lips. She felt fortunate enough to have found a man in tune with life and death like Jonathan was. Someone to make the transition this much more comfortable. It was all luck, really—a roll of the lovers’ dice—the fact that he found her before suicide did.

Nobody understood their relationship, but that didn’t matter. Jonathan was either “too old” or “manipulative.” Just fancy words for what it meant: *I’m jealous of you, Melanie.*

Old angry, bitter bastards.

Jonathan couldn’t—wouldn’t hurt her. He only wanted to protect her, which was what he was doing today—stopping life from sending more of its cruel and unusual punishment her way. But permanently.

No more dealing with parents’ divorce or flunking school exams. No more girls shoving her into metal lockers while laughing like lepers.

He took her hand and began to count. On three, they’d leap to splat together. Melanie bargained for a ten count, but Jonathan said three was perfect. Ten took too long, and one of them might cop out.

So three it was.

One went by quickly. But after two, time rolled over, and Melanie felt every decision in her life bubble up to this exact second. The fear of being alone, from abandonment and death.

When three came sailing out of her lover’s lips, she took her first and last step. Hovering the sole of her shoe above open air, letting the limb know that everything was going to be okay.

And then…Jonathan took his foot off, and Melanie’s world melted like a warm Popsicle.

So she jumped.

But he didn't.

Watching her fall in a top spiral fashion, head over heels, all the way down. No screams or rapid arm flailing, no look of terror of any kind.

Jonathan heard the cement smack from ten stories up, but by then, he was already gone, arms pumping, legs moving in a long horselike stride across the roof. Down through the building staircase and out the back lot.

To be honest, this was the boy's favorite part. He enjoyed it more than picking the girl out and wooing her. More than the moment he knew for sure his victims were committed to him. That they intended to die for him. Melanie hadn't been the first, and most surely wouldn't be the last…

Jonathan was the most renowned heart doctor in the world. And there were a plethora of other patients that needed tending to.

He just had to find them.

Are We Dead Yet?

Susanna set her alarm clock for seven for the seventh time. Praying to God that tomorrow would come and the sun would whisper its gospel through the clouds, telling her that everything was going to be okay.

Even though, deep down in the pit of her heart, she knew things weren't going to be.

The knock on her bedroom window was loud and audacious, and molded by days of knowing unrest and existential terror. It didn't care about the woman's privacy or intimate thoughts. The knock demanded a reply.

Harold Knick wasn't the type of man any woman chooses to spend her last days with. He was big and round with an obnoxiously protruding belly. And messy in a way babies are after devouring dinner; globs of crumbs, leftover food, and snot and drizzle decorated Harold's shirt. Susanna thought he was the grossest man she'd ever met.

"Susie, I think you should reconsider my offer. Suppose things don't...get any better. We're responsible for the repopulation." Harold snorted, no doubt leaving his grubby fingerprints all over the window pane.

"Harold, go away!" Susanna snarled. God—the silly fuck made her feel dirty without doing anything. Like she was a piece of beef on a stick sold at the state fair.

It'd been Harold's bright idea to "reproduce" if no one or nothing came to their rescue. But, aside from the obvious benefits of having sex, Susanna didn't know why he was so keen. They were both dead soon anyway.

The twelve-gauge shotgun on the dresser next to Susanna's bed only spat rock salt. It was one of the few (for reasons unknown) objects that kept waking up with her. Yesterday, the bathroom sink had gone; the day before last, a Mickey Mouse reading lamp Susanna had had since childhood.

Starting the day before, Susanna and Harold kept a recorded track of the items still available. Like nonperishable food items, toothbrushes, undergarments, and the like. Everything else was going, gone. Vanishing into thin air like the a magician's trick.

Harold didn't know about the gun, though.

And with the way he'd had been acting; lately, she had no plans to tell him. It was Susanna's insurance card. One trigger-happy rock salt blast to the face would keep Harold's prick in his pants if he tried anything. Although she hoped it wouldn't have to come to that.

"Okay. But, ah—Susie. I spent all last night on the radio. Still nothing," Harold squeaked.

Susanna sighed. "Go back to your apartment, Harold. Just wait. Someone will come."

"But…what if they don't? What then?"

"Dammit, Harold. Please. Okay. Just go away. I'll talk to you tomorrow." She tossed her bedcover over her head.

But Harold wouldn't quit.

"Susie, I—I had a dream last night. First, my nose slid off my face and shattered on the ground like a ceramics sculpture. But there was no pain! No pain at all. I'm terrified I'll fall apart!" Harold moaned. He was beating his hands on the glass.

Acid tears.

But Susanna didn't reply. She kept the bedcover draped over her body and slept, choosing to ignore all the pain and suffering the outside world offered—including Harold. Curled up in a fetal position with her legs tucked together and only the humming of her heartbeat spoke.

And the days passed by, one after the other, falling in tune like dominos. Morning, noon, and night, the same bedtime nightmare monster with snarling jaws and crooked mandibles. There's no pain or sadness with ignorance, only a melancholia rain shower dancing above one's head.

After a while, Susanna didn't hear from Harold anymore. No more hard knocks or blabbering eulogies about sex, love, and life. Just a quiet, peaceful nothingness.

Deep in her heart, she hoped he suffered before death. If he hadn't killed himself, the "event" had. Watching the flesh drip off his bones like gooey pizza cheese would've been the highlight of her life.

The thought made her crack a gruesome smile, still buried beneath the covers, a monster secluded in its cavern.

Five days later, the tanks rolled in. On top of the machines were men in hazmat suits carrying flamethrowers. Burning to the ground everyone that'd already begun wilting, while lame flower petals drifted down from treetops and soldiers caught them in gloved hands.

Radios belted back and forth as men kicked down doors and torched furniture with missing limbs. And bedposts with no mattresses. And bathroom mirrors with no sinks. Anything to stop the spread of the virus.

Lieutenant Jeffrey James lowered his torch, eyeing a cat skeleton up in an oak tree. Patches of bloody fur stuck to bits of bare rib rack and droopy paws. He thought the poor thing must've caught it and then scaled the tree to die.

Not that the dead cat was a shocker or anything. In the last eight days, James had seen more death than anyone he knew. There was more pain, suffering, and bleakness in the world than it knew what to do with.

Still, their orders were to torch—so they had. Because if the human species is good at anything, it's destroying itself.

Nobody knew where the virus came from or what it was at all. Or why it picked certain people and left others alone. In the incoming decade, there would undoubtedly be studies about the event and what took place. But James was a pessimist. He, like so many other survivors, knew the answers were ghost ships. They'd never come.

He first heard the moans coming from inside the apartment complex, causing him to whip the flamethrower round—finger on the burner trigger.

With each step he took toward the complex, however, the gasps and groans increased. At the same time, pale monsters with shiny yellow teeth picked their gums in his imagination.

"Hello, is anybody in here? If so, come out slowly, please, so I can see you," James hollered. Aching to torch if need be.

When he found which apartment the groans were coming from, he kicked the front door down, splintering wood chips in the process.

Everything in the apartment interior was gone—or dead and rotting. There were no chairs, tables, desks, or anything at all. Just a big empty square with wind tiptoeing through empty cracks in the walls and whistling their dark tunes.

But the groans persisted. They were coming from somewhere deeper in the apartment's belly. Satan's innards.

"Come out now!" James hollered, leveling the flamethrower, feeling a trickle of sweat run down the back of his neck.

The "thing" was huddled underneath piles of overlapping blankets. Shifting and moping alongside the floor in a drunkard's dance. Moving sluggishly toward the young soldier…

James saw bits of choppy slop trailing out from behind the thing as it moved—what looked like an undercooked vegetable stew in a tin pot. Whatever hid beneath the coverall of steaming blankets hiccupped and belched.

He heard more sloshing.

"I'm all better now, I promise," the moving goop mesh growled, the words coming in inconsistent hums.

Plop. Plop. Plop.

But James hit the burner and torched it, unable to look away as the thing belted out a scream, adding more fire and flame to the mix.

While the world carried on.

The Chosen Few

Nothing is a coincidence.

He adjusted the rifle barrel, twisting screws and clanks like clockwork. Leaning on an elbow, his breathing steady, quieter than a grasshopper chirp. Finger wrapped around the trigger—waiting.

Killing feels like the end of November, when the days are wet and cold and the sky is a depressive blue hinge on the edge of madness.

Watching someone's soul slip away isn't for the faint of heart. And it often leads the killer himself to darker thoughts of death and mortality, wondering what it'd feel like if the roles were reversed and they were the ones staring down a black barrel?

Jack didn't know much. But what he did know was that everyone (even atheists) prays when there's a gun pointed at their face.

And for some particular reason, he thought, that was the most disappointing fact of all. Knowing that even in the end, a human being will never be able to rewire their circuitry.

Including himself.

That's why assassins are handpicked early on, usually in childhood, and then guided toward the dark side, fed irrevocable violence until a lust for decadence is instilled in their pea-brained minds.

When Jack was a younger man, seeing other people as objects made it easier to kill. But now? Well, now, with decades of living on the edge, the job only added to his depression, which grew and grew every year like a fungus.

To the sleepless nights.
To the brain fog.
To the overindulgence.
To the next drug, drink, or woman…

But not anymore!

Placing his mouth on the barrel ended up being a lot harder than pulling the trigger, but Jack did it anyway. Sending his soul skyrocketing right to hell.

Blood and brains painted the walls of the child's bedroom in a maroon mist. Gooey red gobs fell from everywhere in between.

The sound was so loud that five-year-old Robbie Hewett bolted up out of bed, eyes bugged out, heart racing, eyeing the bloody mess he used to call his room and the open window (with a minor trickle of warm air cascading in) and the unidentifiable headless stranger who sat on the foot of his bed. Whose upper half looked more squashed fruit than human.

And although Robbie was only five years old, he didn't scream or cry out. He only sat still like a broken record player caught on an endless scratch loop. Skipping over and over and over again.

Robbie's parents were quick, though, bursting into their child's room in an abundant fever. Their pale white moon faces steamed, cooked in madness. Mrs. Hewett began screaming first, louder than any orgasm, injury, or scare life had ever given her, her heart thumping toward hot oblivion.

And her only child was bathed in blood. Not saying one word.

"What happened? Robbie? Oh, God. Who is that!" Mrs. Hewett shouted, scooping their child off the bed and dragging him out of the room while dodging all kinds of horrible thoughts and dive bomber fleets of dread. "Call 911! NOW."

Robbie's father roared. He was already beginning to feel sick. Rumblings of the gunfire echo stewed last night's dinner around in a cocoon.

Mrs. Hewett sobbed uncontrollably while her husband punched in digits with shaky fingers. "Yes! Someone broke into our house and shot themselves! Get over here right away." His voice was raw and unfiltered, like black tar cigarettes.

Meanwhile.

Halfway across town, the emergency operator nodded and took the victim's address. He assured the family that gun-toting lawmen were on their way already.

Which was half true.

Because, when he put the phone down, the masked figure with the pistol silencer pointed at his head smiled brightly.

"We're sending our people—so no need to relay or report this to anyone. What happened tonight is bigger than you, or me, or any of us. We create monsters, and tonight, through an act of beautiful sacrifice to inflict trauma—another seed has been planted. I know none of this makes sense right now. My guess is you'll wonder for the rest of your life about who I am and what I *really* do. Keep it like that. If you go around asking anyone questions—and I mean anyone, your supervisor or whoever—my people will know, and you and your family will be executed."

The operator felt the weight of the gun disappear. And then the figure was gone. A spiderweb of memory already corroding in the dusty moonlight.

The operator hoped the boy would be all right.

The Series Finale

The wineglasses were fat and full like beluga whales. By the night's end, all the bottles lined up on the kitchen counter would be emptied.

They were binge drinkers. Chugging poison with the enthusiasm of schoolchildren huffing candy fumes.

Melinda Richards tipped her glass and downed the wine in one almighty gulp. Her husband, Joss Richards, did the same.

The couple looked good, better than usual. Melinda's hair was poofy perfection, and Joss wore his favorite tie, the one with the piano keys.

"Did you know Ralph Dyer died yesterday?" Joss chirped. His eyes were narrow slits, maybe from all the alcohol—or not. Who really knew?

"Oh, who's that, dear?"

"I went to school with him. The poor bastard blew his brains out. Couldn't wait around for the end like the rest of us."

"Hmm. Ralph from…medical school?" Melinda smirked, her fingernails tap-dancing on the tabletop, moving so quickly that they could've given Michael Jackson a run for his money.

"No, my high school."

"Oh dear, everybody goes there."

"Well, that doesn't make him any less important. Ralph and I grew up together."

"I suppose. Mmm. Is there any more wine?" Melinda slurred, beginning to sway to the music in her head.

"You're an ass. And I hate you when you drink."

"Hmm. Oh, honey, I know that." Melinda giggled, kicking herself off the chair in one mighty leap. Olympic gymnasts would've marveled at how she somehow kept her grace under such conditions.

"Hey! Where are you going!" He belched, and tried to follow her but was too drunk, falling on the floor instead.

"Outsideeeeee!" Melinda cackled, running for the door, stiletto heels thumping the velvet carpet, arms flinging madly.

There was a dead man on the front lawn. A butcher knife stuck out of his back. The knife resembled an enemy flag on the battlefield more than kitchen cutlery. And standing next to the corpse was the killer: a slim woman in a silver dress and with messy hair. Her eyes were pumpkin round—bloodshot and fueled by rage. But Melinda only smiled back, admiring her neighbor's glowing anger. "Thought I'd do the prick in before the bomb did," the skinny woman snarled.

"Well, the amount of times he cheated on you, he deserved it," Melinda quipped. But now she was really beginning to feel it. All the alcohol sloshed over her like a tidal wave, and she fell over in a giggling, snorting heap.

"Do you want me to do Joss too?" the skinny woman howled. She hovered over Melinda's Jell-O frame.

Above their heads, the sky turned a billowy orange that vibrated and glowed like a heartbeat. It was the most beautifully vivid portrait of destruction the world had ever seen.

“Uh…no. Joss was good to me. A doofus. But good.” Melinda got to her feet and giggled again, holding her friend and neighbor in a tight embrace.

The rest of the block was chaos. Fires hissed and flared. People screamed and died by their own hand. Or they killed others—a man in a baker’s outfit was walking around with a frying pan, smacking people on the head till their brains dribbled out. It seemed that nobody wanted to be around—or sane—when the final bomb went off and dusted everything to bits.

“It was Joss’s idea to drink, but I may end up being sick before it’s all said and done,” Melinda hissed, doing everything in her power to fight off the dreaded spins, which were coming in waves now.

“I might go now, Melinda,” the woman said. “It was nice seeing you one last time.” She gripped and ripped the knife out of her husband’s back and left.

A minute later, Joss, bits of food on his chin, was out on the lawn beside his wife, collapsing into a smelly, vomitous heap. “I think I drank too much.”

But Melinda wasn’t even looking at him anymore. Her gaze was gone and distant, lost in the orange bile above their heads. “Do you think it’ll hurt?”

“What’ll hurt?”

“Oh—you know what.”

“Who knows? Now shut up and hold my hand,” Joss hiccupped, wrapping his arm around her like a garden snake.

The pair looked up. And waited.

The Night Sky People

Burnt matches and blackened fingertips from messing around with Satan's pastime. Hollowed-out faces and sunken cheeks crossing lines to sniff lines.

Derelicts by society's standards but compadres within these walls. Everyone in the group took their turn talking, while the others listened with their hands clasped together. They sat still like a metal pole had been ramrodded through each of their spines to keep them upright.

Some were powder junkies, while others couldn't keep their teeth off the bottle like a baby asking for milk.

After class, Eva got in her car, a navy blue Nissan with shiny doors and one window to view the world.

Then she hit the highway, put her foot on the gas, and drove faster, getting as far away from the building as possible.

When they were a mile out, a head poked out of the back seat, sporting a snooty smile and pointed nose.

"Nobody saw you leave with me, so we're good," Eva said, using the rearview mirror to give her partner a sigh.

Kahlo crawled up front and wiggled his furry butt onto the passenger seat. His checkered paw clawed at the belt. The catsuit was rank and dirty, with brown soil smudges on both knees and elbows from crawling around. The man wearing it didn't fare any better. His blubbery chin was littered with the remains of some noodle concoction from leftover takeout food. And when he talked, his breath smelled of warm beer.

Although twenty-three-year-old Eva never inquired about her friend's age, she would have guessed he was probably forty but looked fifty-two. Weathered. Craggy. But functional.

“How was your meeting tonight, cutie?” Kahlo sat back in the passenger seat. He held a tin flask with a screw cap in one hand and would take quick shots every ten seconds or so, throwing his head back and scrunching his polka-dot painted cheeks.

“I don’t like being called ‘cute.’ It’s degrading,” Eva replied. She thought it’d always been strange how older men clung to her like flies on cow shit. She did look young for her age, though, sporting a round baby face and bird’s-chirp smile. Going to bars or restaurants guaranteed a “root around purse searching for ID moment” more often than not.

Especially if she brought Kahlo with her.

“Sorry. Damn. So what are we doing tonight?” Kahlo cackled.

“I don’t know, Kahlo. I have work early tomorrow, can’t be out late—”

But he didn’t seem to care, cutting her off with an extended yawn. “Agh boringgggggg. Let’s go to McGrady’s for a pint.” He gave Eva a sly sneer.

“I’m sober now. We can’t do that, remember?” Eva sighed, her fingers tapping nervously on the steering wheel. She thought the moon above looked pretty tonight, like a real-life oil painting, blurring silvers and dashes of blacks slapped across the canvas.

“Ah, fuck ’em, Evs. We’re the night sky people, God’s unwanted children. We make our own rules.” Kahlo grinned, cracking the window to toss the empty flask out.

“McGrady’s doesn’t want you back. Remember?” Eva gulped.

"Oh, yeah. Well, fuck them. Tell me the law that mandates what people can and cannot wear in public."

"There's actually a few, Kahlo. Remember who you are."

"Whatever." His eyes rolled back.

Eva hated being straightforward with her friend. But sometimes she had to if he got too deep in the fantasy.

The duo couldn't have told you how they met, or where, or which substance they were under at the time. But they'd gotten along like nuts and bolts and looked out for each other ever since.

In the beginning, there were only a couple of rules. One, that Kahlo wouldn't ask Eva to stop drinking or bring the topic of her substance abuse or depression up at any time. And two, she couldn't ever ask him about the cat costume.

Like *why* he wore it. Or what it meant. Or if he ever planned on chucking it.

Some nights, between one beer and the next, Eva felt the courage to drum up a mystery. To boldly go where no one had gone before. But she never did. Instead, Kahlo wore the catsuit, and she drank. Downing glass after glass effortlessly, like an assassin loading a gun.

They both did.

They were the Night Sky People.

At first, everyone assumed the duo were freaks. Lovers. Role-playing some schoolgirl/bed wetter kink in real life. Her, looking as young as she did, and he, a sweaty overweight weirdo with uncontrollable lust.

But Kahlo had never—not once—come on to her, even when, in some toxic whirlwind stupor, she wanted him to. The drink had a way of awakening the loneliness in her soul like a spider slinging a web.

"What's gotten into you?" Kahlo quipped.

"Huh? What do you mean?" Eva couldn't help but bite her lip in hesitation. A part of her knew what was coming…

"You're not fun anymore. And we barely go out, and if you do hit me up, nothing happens."

"I—I've been busy. You know about the classes."

"Stop going to them, then."

"You know I can't do that, Kahlo."

"Then, I guess I'll have to quit you." Kahlo shrugged, his shoulders slumping in exhausted defeat.

"What? No, you can't do that!" Eva spat back. She could feel the ever-pounding thump of her heart picking up speed.

"I can do whatever I want. Always have. But…pull over at the next bus stop." Kahlo coughed, unable to look at her anymore. His gaze shot past her toward the empty road ahead.

Eva tried to hold back the tears as best she could, but they came pouring out like waterworks nevertheless, down onto her breasts and lap.

The bus stop was disgusting. Sticky gum paper everywhere and wads of balled-up trash next to an empty bin. Next to said bin was a random abandoned shopping cart taking a smoke break—left behind by some junkie. Every city corner has one, but only a few shine like a lighthouse beacon above the rocks.

When Eva pulled the car over, a piano dinged in the sky—playing its melancholy tune for all to hear.

They were alone.

"Please don't leave me," she whispered—hot tears scalding the mounds of her cheeks—overflowing aqueducts of pain and turmoil.

"Who said I'm the one leaving?" Kahlo whispered back. A trace of venom lay in each syllable.

"Huh? What?" Eva coughed. Feeling vulnerable when he leaned across—stopping one inch from her face. And touched her nose with his...

"Get out," he said, palming her back against the door with his paws.

"Kahlo?"

"Bye-bye!" Kahlo howled. And struck her across the face. Not once, but twice, then three times. In retaliation, Eva jerked the door handle and flung herself out. Doing anything she could to escape the onslaught of her friend's fists coming at supersonic speed.

She rolled out onto the street, collecting bumps, rashes, and tangled mess of hair, snot, slime, and tears too.

The car took off, shooting bits of gravel and murk her way in splintered pieces, before the girl had the chance to look up.

Eva covered her face and began to cry. She didn't know how long she lay there. It could've been a minute or ten. But for however long it was, the spot was her sanctuary.

Soaking everything in.

The wheels of a rusty car boomed in the background, jarring her to awareness. So Eva wiped her face and squinted hard, catching the outline of a lonely figure headed toward her. Thin and shapely, with a tattered rag sheet cast over its body.

“Hello?” Eva said, beginning to pick herself up.

The man in the dog costume was younger than Kahlo, maybe thirty. And in better shape too. With a bright, beaming smile and a collar wrapped around his neck.

“Hey there. You doing okay, girl?” Dogman barked, noticing her tears and snot now.

“Yeah. I’m okay…I guess. Who are you?”

“Call me Spike. Do you live around here? Ain’t ever seen you before.”

“No, I…no, I don’t actually.”

“Mm. Well, the next bus doesn’t come till sunrise so…would you like company?” When Dogman talked, his ears perked up and a bell on his collar jingle-jangled.

Eva sighed. And forced herself to smile. She found it easier than she would have thought.

“Yeah, I’d like that.”

Almost Famous

The alarm went off at seven. School began at eight. He had an hour to get ready, shower, comb his hair, brush his teeth, put on clothes, and load the bullets into the chamber of the handgun.

Six rounds that would pump out like bombs. Boom. Boom. Boom. Boom. Boom. Boom. Blood. Brains. Guts. Swine.

He had to tell himself to slow down, to stop and smell the roses. Or all the meticulous planning would be for nothing.

"Okay, remember the road map," Alistair Lowe said while tucking the pistol in the waistband of his jeans. Nobody could see it, which was just the way he planned.

The fourteen-year-old missed Mom's breakfast and the bus on purpose, choosing instead to walk the way on an empty stomach. Every lurch and growl was a tiger hidden behind the jungle folds.

I wonder if they'll ever know? Probably not. Alistair chuckled to himself, thinking about all the news coverage. There would be a thousand interviews with his family members, friends, cousins, other relatives. All asking the same question.

Why?

The word *why* keeps the world spinning. It gets people out of bed to work and to pay the bills to keep on…living. But for what? For who? Why do anything at all if you're owed a toe tag?

From time to time, Alistair pondered some of life's biggest questions, never thinking that one day history's biggest *why* would be about him.

Why would a seemingly normal suburban kid shoot and kill his own classmates? Randomly—and without remorse.

And pop himself in the head when it's all said and done. Alistair smiled. He loved the feeling of his cheeks stretched all the way back.

The suburbs.

The empty morning sky echoed back with sounds of bird chirps, and brown branches swayed in the gentle breeze. Freshly cut grass and manicured lawns decorated the countryside, easing the day onward and upward. Alistair enjoyed the walk to school. Knowing that it'd be his last was bittersweet, but thrilling also. Everything seemed brighter, more vibrant, and in tune with the fairytale in his head.

Death would come easy (and, he prayed, painless) and the darkness would settle in like a baby in its crib. Alistair shut both eyes and shook hands with afterlife, doing everything and anything he could to welcome it. *But my legacy will live on for generations to come. I'll be...famous.*

Alistair opened his eyes again and tugged on the pistol. By now, it'd grown on him. Almost like a third arm. He felt more comfortable with it than he did with any notebook or pen.

Twenty minutes later, Alistair was trotting through his school parking lot. Crooked grin. Hand on the gun's grip. God, it was happening, *really* happening now. Everything he'd dreamed about for months.

He was so close.

You've practiced this, he told himself. *You know the exits. Go around back through the lunchroom double doors. Slip in quietly—everyone's in homeroom. And then...pick a class. Any class. And go off. But just remember to leave one in the chamber for yourself. You're a martyr, the messiah of death, and what you're about to do will be talked about for a century.*

So the boy told himself. Savoring every word like a sweet dessert. So, so very close now…OH GOD.

"Hey, Alistair, can I quote you for the yearbook?" someone chirped. The speaker was a tallish, long-haired, dirty-eyed sophomore named Tom Wright. Wright stopped in front of Alistair and smiled, huffing and out of breath. There was a pen and notebook in one of his hands, and a Nikon camera in the other. A hall pass badge stapled to his shirt said COLUMBINE HIGH SCHOOL YEARBOOK STAFF PHOTOGRAPHER.

"Huh? What—no, Tom, go away." Alistair noticed the kid's red eyes. He looked high. Which probably wasn't that much of a surprise, considering it was 4/20. The stoners' holiday…

"Agh, come on, man!" Wright cackled, beginning to follow Alistair into the building, trailing him like a lapdog.

"Goddammit, Tom! Didn't you hear me—"

Alistair didn't get to finish his sentence. The alien boom that thundered down the hallway whipped both of the boys around, stopping them in their tracks.

"What was that?" Tom whispered.

They heard another roar of gunfire. This one closer than the last. Pow. Pow. Pow. Semiautomatic rifles belly-laughing.

A cascade of students and teachers sprinted down the hall toward them, hands and feet pumping like crazy.

Tom and Alistair were both pushed out by the tidal wave of people running for their lives. Sneakers, backpacks, basketball shoes.

"Hey! What's going on—ugh—agh—hey!" Alistair shouted, nearly tossed to the floor by the stampede of human buffalo.

Pow. Pow. Pow.

But nobody cared—they just kept running.

Except for one person, a short, round, fat junior with pigtails named Shirley Burton. Tears dribbled down her stumpy chin. "Someone's shooting in the library! Get the fuck out!" she screamed, grabbing Alistair by the arm and dragging him back outside. He followed, mouth hanging open, eyes dilated in shock.

Alistair stood out on the grass in front of the school with everyone until the police (clad in SWAT gear and with weapons of their own) and ambulance arrived. Every five to ten minutes, he heard a gunshot go off or someone crying out for help.

An hour later, the shooting stopped, and the word was that the trigger men had been stopped too.

A couple hours after that, Alistair was back home again, where his mother and father hugged him tighter than ever before. Crying. Rejoicing.

And a couple hours after *that*, Alistair was in bed, the gun tucked safely under his mattress. He exhaled, letting loose a gust of frustrated air.

Maybe next time.

The Beautiful People

It was one of those shitty motels. You know, the kind with cum stains and bullet holes. A place rancid runaways flee to like a fairytale.

The woman knew that the end of civilization was nothing more than cheap sex and faucet taps that dispensed brown liquid.

She checked in at noon, got her card key and room number, and sat tight. The day manager who checked her in, some rusty old fuck with two felonies and a pending sexual assault case on his record, didn't notice or care because the woman hid under thick layers of clothing and messy makeup. To anyone else, the woman was just another freak staying at freak city. A nobody, a nothing.

But in the woman's profession, being invisible was akin to oxygen—one can't stay alive without it.

She carried an ugly plastic suitcase with her. After she'd checked into the room and bolted the door and shut the window curtains, she threw the suitcase on the bed and began to peel off clothing like onion layers. Trench coat, undercoat, undercoat under the undercoat, an undershirt, two padded bras, and a pair of oversized men's jeans. All in all, it took her twenty minutes to become beautiful again.

Underneath, she was young and slim, with thick shoulder-length black hair and dark eyes to rival the night sky.

Thirty minutes later, however, there was a knock at the door. A mountain of a man. He was big, fat, tall, and ugly. Maybe six four. Three hundred pounds. He had an oily complexion and thinning hair that hung down on his forehead in dewy clumps.

When she saw him, something inside her growled like a tiger in the jungle. “Shut it behind you and bolt the lock. I don’t want anyone interrupting us,” she said.

So he did. Enveloping the both of them in a black iron shadow.

“Now, remove your clothes. But do it…slowly,” the woman barked, her naked breasts heaving up and down with each syllable, a single trickle of sweat running down her back.

It took the man five minutes to strip, removing layer after layer. A thick snowplower’s coat, seven wool knit sweaters, six long-sleeve T-shirts, five short-sleeve T-shirts, four pairs of pants, three pieces of underwear, and one pair of combat boots with a four-inch vertical lift inserted into the heel. Then his face prosthetics—bits of synthetic plastic and dabs of makeup.

Underneath the warlock wig and costume was a different man, one with slicked-back hair and razor-blade cheekbones, a lean torso and sinewy muscles. An artist’s conception of the perfect male with no flaws.

The two beautiful people admired one another for the longest moment. Their eyes interlocked in a secret love language not even the stars could interpret.

“You’re gorgeous. It’s been a while since I’ve seen somebody like you,” the woman whispered, running her smooth hands across his body, every divot and slope.

“You too. But now we must discuss the mission at hand.” He flashed a pearly-white million-dollar smile.

“What were your orders?”

"Same as yours. Make contact, destroy the premises. And then, rendezvous at the pickup tomorrow morning," he said, moving past her to search the room. "Where are the guns? We'll need them. The Uglies won't lay down and die, you know."

"In the suitcase I brought. There's some knives in there too." The woman picked up a knife by the rubber-covered grip; its shiny silver blade reflected light on her beautiful face. "And a couple of hand grenades."

Outside in the parking lot, a car whipped in, its tires flinging up dust, dirt, and smoke. There was the sound of a door opening—rusted over by years of grease buildup and negligence.

"Check it out. Make sure we weren't being followed!" the man said. He grabbed a gun and began to load hollow points into the chamber.

She peeped the blinds a teeny-tiny fraction, one perfectly manicured fingernail doing the job. She exhaled. "We're good. It's just some guy and a hooker. Two lonely souls intertwined for the moment."

"Ugly?"

"Yeah, they're overweight. Probably have bad odor and poor overall hygiene too," she quipped, shutting the window blind before someone spotted her and alerted the authorities. "Are we killing everyone?"

"Total"—he cocked a gun—"wipeout. You heard about the ambush at Silverdale Mall in California, right?"

"Yeah. How many of our people were shot?"

"Everyone. No survivors."

"How…how does that even happen?" the woman gasped. Her cheeks were cold and pale like a lonely astronaut circling space. Distant and forgotten.

"I heard it was at a suit store in the mall where they sell real fancy imported shit from Europe. Leather belts, suede shoes, stuff like that. The ugly bastards have gotten smarter—or a better fashion sense. Which I don't think is the case." He tossed her a pistol and began walking toward the door. She followed. "Remember, shoot to kill, darling. In this war, there are no prisoners."

And the beautiful people, their jawlines sharp as knives, stepped outside. A sliver of bright vibrant sun hit their perfectly tanned and toned skin just right.

Thirty seconds later, the screaming started.

Old

The end of the world isn't fire and brimstone or devils holding pitchforks. It isn't earthquakes and screaming babies, collapsed civilizations, or death to all.

The end of the world is more quiet and subdued—personal. Because the end of the world is different for every individual. One man's heaven is another's hell.

Ralph Roberts's biggest fear was being stuck and ending up alone. And now the irony was that he couldn't go anywhere if he tried.

So when the little girl showed up, he saw the sun through the clouds for the first time in what felt like forever. The girl was ten or so, with a pair of pigtails and wearing a strawberry-colored dress. And the tag wrapped around her neck read: *For Ralph, keep out of trouble.*

Ralph eyed the android on his doorstep with a high level of interest, his mouth cocked into a grisly grin. His arms were folded together, big things with tattoos of a panther on one and a fish hook on the other. Compliments of a youth spent in the Navy.

And, although Ralph was nearing seventy, he still had the strength of a man twenty years his junior. One of the few old-fashioned iron-and-grit types still kicking—the kind that pisses lightning and roars thunder.

The girl didn't weigh that much, maybe forty pounds, making it easy to carry her inside and bolt the lock. When Ralph scooped her up, though, he could hear the nuts and bolts rattling on the inside, jingling like dimes in a washing machine. This only made his smile broader.

"Wake up, sleepy," Ralph snickered, slapping the tin bot upside her head. Not in a cheeky reminder sort of way, but coldly and aggressively.

When the thing opened her eyes and stared back at him, he didn't flinch, however. He only winked back in return. "Morning, darling, welcome to your new home," he said, chalky white spittle collecting at either side of his mouth. Building and bubbling up.

This one was a lot prettier than all the other models in the magazine. There was an innocence about this one, a kindness behind the eyes—if that was even possible for a machine.

And already he felt a growling wolf deep in his loins, howling at the moon, happy and ecstatic that its meal had finally arrived.

He looked down at the beeping red ankle monitor wrapped around his limb and sighed, wanting to burn the damn thing off like an Alabama tick. Every morning and night, the thing itched, chafing the skin and causing little bright bumps. "Only one hundred and eighty-six more days of you," he grunted. Trying not to think about the day he'd finally be off house arrest. How that would be.

Like a shot of adrenaline to the heart.

The girl's name was Cherry. Model number 464478. Ralph wondered if the numbers meant anything particular or were just there for speculation. It didn't matter; she was still the most beautiful little girl he'd ever seen.

Or felt.

Her arm was soft and meaty, like a real human arm. And warm too, with artificial liquid coloring pumping through plastic veins.

Ralph rubbed a spot on the girl's arm and smiled, feeling the happiest he'd felt in years. A total oneness with somebody—something. Anything at all.

"The only regret I have is you that weren't legal when I was a lot younger! We could've had a lot of fun together." Ralph snickered while reaching his hand underneath the android's strawberry bubblegum dress.

Just a little sneak. One finger in the wire mesh to taste for himself.

When the phone rang, he jerked his head up—snarling, huffing, caught up.

"Hmm. Ralph Roberts speaking," he said, one hand cradling the receiver like a baby.

"Hey, Ralphie, how do you like her?" someone cackled on the other end. Their breathing heavy in anticipation.

"She's cute. But I haven't turned her on yet," Ralph replied.

"Well, go on and have some fun. But don't be afraid to tell us what you think later on. You're one of the first felons to participate in our program," the voice chirped.

"Get this fucking bracelet off my leg, and you're a genius," Ralph hiccupped, using his other leg to scratch the tagged one.

"That's impossible, bud."

He sighed. "The girl told me she was eighteen—"

But the voice cut Ralph off. Slicing through the phone line like a samurai sword into butter. "I've heard it all before, Mr. Roberts. And frankly, I don't care. All my company does is offer an...alternative therapy. Signed, stamped, and approved by Johnny Law, of course."

"I'm not a monster."

"No, Mr. Roberts, you're just sick."

"So, what do you think happens to me after this?"

"I think…there is no after for you, Mr. Roberts. Have a nice day." And with a click, the raspy voice was gone—a ghost in the wind of time.

Leaving convicted felon Ralph Roberts standing alone in his kitchen.

"'There is no after'?" He smirked and slammed the phone back on the receiver. What an asshole. Fuck him.

The knock on the front door was loud. Booming like a rock drum in a small club. *Bang. Bang. Bang.* One after another.

But Ralph Roberts didn't move aside from subconsciously leaning all his weight on one leg defiantly. Waiting like a child, hoping the noise would grow tired and wander away.

Bang. Bang.

"Fuck...okay," Ralph spat. He hobbled on toward the door, right past the girl. Her lifeless mechanical eyes were two pin drops in an aluminum bucket.

However, when Ralph opened the door, the thing that stood before him was anything but lifeless.

The bot's shoulders were broad and proud like two mountaintops. And unlike the girl, he was male and a bit bigger than Ralph, which made his domineering presence more frightening.

And this one had been switched on.

"Christ. They made others too?" Ralph was unable to do or say much of anything with valor or grit. The control he'd felt with the girl was gone now.

"Ralph Roberts. I'm here for the second phase of your alternative therapy," the bot sang. Electrical wire jingle-jangled and hot sparks flared as it talked.

"Wh-what is this? No! Who are you, who sent you here?"

But the bot was more robust than Ralph, and made its way into his home with one sturdy push.

Then, Ralph saw the leather belt and lighter in its hand.

"I'm her father, Mr. Roberts." Mr. Bot cracked a grin like a beer can and took one artificial step forward, metal clanking against the floor.

And for Ralph Roberts, there was indeed…no after.

No Refund Policy

"Someone go get Violet and bring her down here," William Hill instructed. The words floated from his soft lips like music notes. Calming but orderly.

Hill, the group's commander in chief, was clad in black from neck to toe, including shiny satin black gloves and round bubble bug protective eyewear over both eyes.

He looked more Liberace than metaphysical guru.

The rest of his followers—men and women, old, young, short, fat, fit, all different types of meat vessels—sat around a brown oak dinner table with icy wine goblets in front of them. The temptation to drink was etched on their desperate wet-clay faces.

One of the women, fat with swirly dimples and bright blue eyes, excused herself and walked upstairs, her clumpy heels thumping on the steps.

Nine-year-old Violet Hill heard the knock on the bedroom door and looked up, pausing her Candy Crush game for the moment. She had freckled cheeks, a bow in hair, glittery fingernails.

"Violet, we're ready for you downstairs," the fat woman's nervous voice whispered through a crack in the door, the voice's pink tongue and lips wiggling like a worm caught on a fishing line.

In the dining room, a couple of the followers reached under the table and linked hands, locking their fingers and whatever hope they had left into one big fleshy beast.

“I left my job and quit my family for this,” one said out loud. There was a proud, beaming smile stapled to her lips.

“I burned down my house,” another replied, with tears of joy running down his cheeks.

“We are the chosen ones!” a couple laughed together. An almighty roar of approval rose from the other followers.

William Hill clapped and moved his bug-eyed goggles to the top of his shiny bald head. “Indeed! And tonight, AS I PROMISED YOU ALL, the prophet will lead everyone to the holy land where a mecca of prosperity and enlightenment awaits you all!” He roared, “How many of you have ever wanted to talk to God? Well, tonight, The Goddess of The Garden in HERE with us. And HER name…is Violet!”

All heads turned toward the end of the table, where a little girl in a dress the color of strawberry jam sat with a phone in her hand, obviously too invested in her game to care about much about anything else going on.

“Violet? Creator of the universe?” one member said, biting his lower lip to stop it from trembling.

But William spoke for her.

“Yes, Violet is her earthbound name. But you also know her as the Messiah, or Muhammad, or Buddha, or Jesus Christ. Life began with her, and it shall end too.” He smiled, extending his arms high into the air.

“Oh…brilliant! Praise God!” a follower said, and began to pray with his head pressed firmly on the tabletop.

“Hallelujah!” Burnt House chirped.

“Does Violet speak?” a woman cried. She seemed unable to stop the tears from flowing.

William turned and directed his warm smile toward his daughter. "Violet, would you be so kind as to say something to the group?"

Not looking up, and obviously still heavily invested in Candy Crush, Violet said, "Oh hey, what's up, guys?"

But everyone at the table practically jumped out of their seats anyhow.

"Oh my Lord! Oh praise the Lord! She speaks," they all howled, clutching each other's shaky, thin, goose bump–covered limbs.

"You have all HEARD the VOICE of your creator! But the question is…WILL YOU hand yourself over to her NOW?" William shrieked, his tongue poking out, eyes bulging out of their sockets. Lost in a yellow honey river of sparkling fish and smiling sailors.

"YES! YES!" everyone bellowed.

"Then, pick up your wine cups and CHEERS to eternity!" William slammed his fists on the tabletop as he watched each and every one of his followers tilt their cups and swallow the toxic drain cleaner in one fell swoop. No hesitation, no worry.

Gulp.

All William could do was smirk, pulling the edges of his lips all the way back into an evil grin.

"Now, everyone, take your BLINDFOLDS off and walk hand in hand into the light with your creator," he whispered, and took a seat.

He watched each and every one of them reach behind their heads and tug the double-knotted bandanas off…

This was always his favorite part.

Usually, there were two groups of people. Those who, on seeing the little girl with the lollipop in her mouth:

were speechless themselves—their expressions colder than ice cubes

or

bolted upright to scream as foam, spittle, and madness coursed through their bones.

Burnt House and Job Quitter responded first, both wobbling up with eyes bugged out. "What…what the fuck is this. A little girl?" Burnt House croaked, white, pasty foam already beginning to bubble from his lips.

"Where is SHE?"

"IS THIS A JOKE?"

"William, William, William!"

But William Hill wasn't having any of it. He exhaled and rolled both eyes back. "No refund policy, people," he snarled. "Now will you all just shut up and die already?"

Burnt House, however, had just enough life force left to charge the table. He rolled himself onto the tabletop on all fours, worming his way toward William as blue veins popped out everywhere in a particularly ugly fashion. "Agh! Aghhhh! You fuck ahh!" he grunted before collapsing dead on the tabletop like a Christmas turkey.

The others followed, some hurling bucketsful of blood and guts onto the carpet; it looked like slop from a pig pen.

Five minutes later, William and Violet were up and picking the followers' pockets for their wallets, flipping open billfolds and taking whatever was inside. Cash, credit cards, anything.

"How much this time, sweetie?" he said, stuffing wads of green bills into his pockets.

"Hmm, I got a couple hundred."

"Yeah, me too. Bunch of broke dickheads." William laughed as he stepped over entangled limbs, arms, legs, and necks.

"Next time!"

"Definitely."

On their way out, William kicked one of his followers in the gut and then bent over and whispered, "Thanks for hosting, asshole."

And daddy and daughter strolled right out the front door.

Honor Killed the Samurai

Stephen peered through the crusty film that covered his eyeballs: a murky late-night spiderweb concoction of dirt, dust, and dry powder.

The bedroom was quiet except for the spinning sound of the ceiling fan, which moaned and gasped like a woman's orgasm in the pale moonlight.

His wife was rolled over on her side, though. Still drifting through a dreamy star system called REM sleep, not a care in the world except her own. Stephen admired the way his wife ignored him. Yes, they'd been married for eleven years, and yes, eleven years seemed like an eternity to some, but to others, it was a finger-snap.

All thoughts and feelings necessary, though. Stephen's jealousy, hatred, and anger toward his wife had boiled up for so long that he thought he'd pop. But he didn't; instead, he clung to the dark dream and held on for dear life.

In Japan, young samurai start training when they're given their first training sword (made of bamboo) at the age of three. But then, anywhere between the age of five and six, they're handed a real weapon—the mamori-gatana sword—able to slice through flesh and blood like warm butter and behead enemies with a single swoop.

So, Stephen slowly got himself out of bed. The wooden floorboards were chilly under his bare toes, creaking beneath the weight of human presence.

The mamori-gatana sword was hidden under the bed, in a creamy white wrap. When Stephen bent over to retrieve it, he also chucked his pajamas and stood nude in the silver slits piercing through the bedroom curtains.

Stephen's sword only weighed two pounds, so it was easy to swing the weapon around and loosen the muscles in his back and shoulders, slicing the air while dancing on tiptoes.

The kimono was in the back of his closet, hanging next to a pair of ironed work pants and a tie he wore to the office in his everyday life. But the kimono looked vastly different: a white skirt sheath with a round belt and blue top. Easy for hopping around or jumping from one platform to another.

Slipping the thing on felt like adding a second layer of skin. Stephen could've been born in it. Umbilical cord cut and bathed with it too. He felt like God, the Pope, Mohammed, and Machine Elf all rolled into one.

Not bad for a late-night Amazon purchase.

While Stephen left the apartment his wife continued to exist in her human hyperbaric chamber. Rolling over once or twice to catch the cool side of the pillow but nothing else. Any other man in the universe would call her the most beautiful creature of all time and space.

Next door, the mamori-gatana cut through their neighbor's neck and severed the head. Quick wisp of adrenaline followed by a curdled scream. No pain in execution.

Then, Stephen carried the head by a clump of hair. Holding it like a gift from God to the Prophet.

He set the head next to his wife's head and let its blood soak the pillow. Red goose feathers look a lot like bird talons in the dark.

Downstairs the phone call took no effort. Dial 9-1-1. Press device to ear, sheath sword, and wait.

"Hello, 911, what is your emergency?"

"Yes, I just witnessed a murder."

"Okay, sir, explain the situation as best you can."

"I just caught my wife in bed with another man. She was giving him head when I killed him."

Till Death Do Us Part

Everyone wears their broken dreams like badges. But only a few can hide their nightmares.

The shed was ten by ten, a delicate little thing with thin but sturdy tuna can tin walls.

It looked like something out of a gothic horror novel, though, with wicked green ivy running up and down its body like spider veins. Whatever secrets it had consumed remained within.

Shelby O'Brien lit her umpteenth cigarette of the day and took a drag, shucking off every jib of worry that'd jabbed her nonstop for the last year.

"God, if you're up there listening now, kill me now," the forty-one-year-old mother of two croaked. She felt every bit of middle age in her tight neck and back. But no rogue bolt of lightning shot down from the sky, nor some unexplainable random plane fuselage doomed to crush her. Nothing happened except for Shelby's ongoing existence.

The bolt cutters in her hands were big enough to break the lock on the shed, to snap it in half and free whatever dark secrets remained within.

Shelby's husband had been a beast of a man. Big, tall, wide, and devilishly insincere. Stoned faced, too. In fact, the only way a smile might've graced his face would've been by force—or by someone armed with a carving knife.

So Shelby shut her eyes and went to her quiet place: a locked box that only she had the key to. Preparing mentally for what had to be done…

"I swear on everything, Jake, if you hurt those girls…" she cried, clamping the bolt cutter's jaws around the lock's torso.

Biting down hard.

The lock gave way and dropped to the ground, slipping into a puddle of steel chain at her feet.

WAIT—don't do this. Just back up, go to the hardware store, and buy another chain. Nobody will ever know, Shelby's inner dialogue whispered back as tears cascaded down her cheeks in silvery rainbows.

Here were eighteen years of a *good* marriage, her identity, and the will to live during that time—about to tumble headfirst into Hell's hot abyss.

"I was good to you, Shelby," her dead husband's voice boomed. It was brittle like a kitchen sponge, soaking up every bit of hope she had. Although the bastard had been gone for two months now, his presence still haunted her mind and soul.

Shelby tossed the bolt cutters aside and began to pry the rusty door open; grey tin scraped against clumpy concrete.

The stench of the corpses was overwhelming. And the whirlpool of flies that blew out from the dark like a shotgun didn't try to hide anything either. Putrid whiffs of yellow piss, hard-crusted brown slop shit, and black flays of decayed flesh painted a portrait.

Shelby caught the sledgehammer softball in her throat, forcing any undigested food back down in a swirly gulp.

“Oh God, Jake. What have you done to me?” She lurched, the anxiety and spiral comet of fear taking over. Gone were the vivid memories of their love painted in her mind, oil portraits with cherry sunsets and white picket fences.

Shelby recognized some of the bodies. Not the girls personally but their school uniforms, which hung in shredded tatters. All private schools from around the tri-state area.

A note had been stapled to one girl’s breasts. It looked more like a laundry list than a confession letter, but Shelby knew what it was right away. Jake always had the best handwriting. It was handsome and daring, but beautiful.

Shelby, if you’re reading this, the cancer has metabolized to my liver, and I’m already dead. But I have a lot to tell you, more time than the world will allow. So find somewhere to sit, and let’s begin...

The note went on for another page, but Shelby didn’t bother to read it. Instead, she smiled briefly, wiped a streak of green snot and tears off her face, and stuffed the letter in her pants pocket. Burying it with…everything else.

So.

She let the shed devour her, walking in and dragging the doors closed until nothing remained but a slice of afternoon light slipping through.

The odor was unbearable until she breathed through her mouth and sucked in mounds of air like candy. Learning to enjoy the process without impurity.

Flies. Rotting, pus-drenched flesh. Blackened liver spots. Enough dead to give the Grim Reaper a hard-on. Her tomb.

Followed by a phone call.

Shelby punched in her neighbor's number.

"Hello, Mrs. Roberts. It's Shelby O'Brien from next door. I'm going away for a while to get my head right. With Jake and the funeral—well, it's all been too much. Would you mind doing something for me? I've already left for the airport, and I forgot to chain up my back shed! I feel so dumb and clumsy asking you, but if a squirrel or other animal gets in, it'll be a mess! Could you stop by the hardware store and then come over and lock the shed up? I'll reimburse you for the chain when I get back."

Shelby spoke so quickly that she barely comprehended the words as they shot out of her mouth. But the Roberts were kind and generous type. Real homemakers—white-picket-fence, till-death-do-us-part people.

Jake had always liked them too.

It took another thirty seconds of talking before Eleanor Roberts agreed to help Shelby out, ticking through the cliché "Well, you look out for yourself, sweetie" conversation any decent human being would have with another during a situation like this.

"Okay, thank you, Eleanor. This means a lot."

She ended the call. And then she went and sat down on her haunches, not far from the nearest corpse. To rest.

Pretty soon, that'd be all she *could* do. She told herself she wouldn't kick, scream, or shout after Eleanor bolted the chain on. No matter what her survival instincts said.

Some secrets were worth taking to the grave.

About the Author

Kyler Jones is the author of *Insomnia Café*. He lives in Connecticut. You can catch more of his work on Instagram: afterdark_no_dreaming13

www.ingramcontent.com/pod-product-compliance
Lightning Source LLC
LaVergne TN
LVHW090949080826
845145LV00003B/947